In the Country of the Young

In the Country of the Young

Stories by
Daniel Stern

SOUTHERN METHODIST
UNIVERSITY PRESS
Dallas

These stories are works of fiction. Names, characters, places, and incidents are either the product of the author's imagination or are used fictitiously.

Requests for permission to reproduce material from this work should be sent to:
  Rights and Permissions
  Southern Methodist University Press
  PO Box 750415
  Dallas, Texas 75275-0415

Some of the stories in this collection appeared first in other publications: "Lunch with Gottlieb," "Time Will Tell," and "Imperato Placeless" in *Hampton Shorts*; "In the Country of the Young" in *Boulevard*; "Chaos" in *The East Hampton Star*; and "Comfort" in *American Short Fiction*.

Jacket art by Vige Barrie
Jacket and text design by Tom Dawson

LIBRARY OF CONGRESS CATALOGING-IN-PUBLICATION DATA

Stern, Daniel, 1928-
    In the country of the young : stories / by Daniel Stern.— 1st ed.
       p. cm.
    Contents: Lunch with Gottlieb — Apraxia — Foxx hunting — Comfort — Imperato placeless — Chaos — Messenger — The exchange — Time will tell — The #63 bus from the Gare de Lyon — In the country of the young.
    ISBN 0-87074-457-7 (alk. paper)
    I. Title.
PS 3569.T3887 I6 2001
813'.54—dc21   00-045025

Printed in the United States of America on acid-free paper

10   9   8   7   6   5   4   3   2   1

To Frank Kermode

And for
Elaine Cali and David and Alexandra Wax

Contents

Lunch with Gottlieb

I begin my education in Moss Gottlieb's elevator in a grungy building on East 54th Street between a Japanese restaurant and a funeral parlor, an elevator filled with the odor of cooking rice and wilting flowers. But this is no ordinary conveyance with proper starts and stops, whizzing up and down a tube of elegant city air. This is the elevator which leads to Moss Gottlieb's office; a dilapidated elevator possessed by a dybbuk (one of the many, to me, exotic Jewish images I will pick up that first New York summer). It moans and shakes every inch of the way, terrorizing its passengers with the threat of eternal entrapment, and when stalled shoots off a clangorous alarm bell from hell; an elevator out of Dante rather than the glamorous universe of advertising agencies which I have come north to discover. I am twenty-three, come to be a Columbus of commerce or literature; the choice is mine, or so I think. Here I am, a flag sent to find a heroic staff from which to fly, only to find myself stalled in Moss Gottlieb's elevator.

When I'm at last released from the Inferno, I find myself facing the sixth floor receptionist.

"My name is Graff," I say.

1

"Yes?"

"Gordon Graff." I add a name; perhaps two might carry more weight.

"Yes?"

"I've just arrived—I'm originally from Richmond, now I live in Daytona." Why my place of birth or present residence would move matters forward is not exactly clear. I am numb from the wet heavy heat, not at my most lucid.

"Mr. Gottlieb?" I try once more.

"Yes?"

"I have an appointment with him. Mr. Moss Gottlieb."

I have now told her all I know in the world, this exhausted morning; that I am Gordon Graff and that I am to meet Moss Gottlieb. The rest is silence. The young woman sitting at the switchboard, all auburn hair and indifference, stares at me. Then, as if I had said a magic word, she comes alive.

"Oh, my God," she says. "You must be the kid—Maria!" She shouts the name. Then: "You're late."

"For what?"

"The lunch. You're supposed to be at the Palm. It's twelve-thirty."

"I know what time it is. I've been stuck in your elevator for ten minutes." Patience, a style of dealing with crises which my father had taught me was a southern value, is becoming a casualty of confusion and fatigue.

"I didn't hear the alarm bell."

"You're lucky. I may never hear again."

"What?"

"And nobody told me I had a lunch date with Mr. Gottlieb."

"It's with the client."

Maria appears. Stocky, Italian, light brown hair; she reminds me of the middle-aged women who are part-time saleswomen at neighborhood stores in Richmond or Daytona. The phone buzzes.

"M and M Advertising." The switchboard operator sounds almost interested.

"Hello," I say to Maria. "I'm Gordon Graff. From Daytona."

But all her agitated attention is devoted to the incoming call.

"Is it him?" she asks the auburn hair. "How does he sound? Is he making sense?"

"It's not him. It's the *New York Times*."

"Thank God. Then he hasn't started yet. Tell them I'm out. Tell them our normal billing period starts the first of July."

Maria is now available to pay attention to me. A quick, shrewd look and I have passed inspection—by what standards I have no idea. I have the impression that what matters to her at this moment is satisfying herself that she will not have to deal with any surprises from me.

"He didn't tell you about the lunch date?"

"Mr. Gottlieb? I've never spoken to him. I have a letter from my uncle—"

"It figures. We'd better get you down right away. Moss needs you. Don't worry. It's only a matter of life and death." She shakes her head—a mother bemused by the foolishness of a child. "Never told him about lunch with Steinardt. What a hot sketch. You know the Palm?"

"I've never been to New York before."

"Oh, Jesus. Then Jessica can take you. Jessica! Jessica! Why the fuck is her door closed in the middle of the work day?"

"She's meditating," the Switchboard says. "Check the note on the door." The only closed door on the floor does indeed carry a printed legend: Meditation in Progress. Please Do Not Disturb Between Twelve and One.

The Italian woman tears the paper from the door. But she does not open or knock. "Shit," she murmurs. She squares off her chin. "I'm going to tell Moss she's meditating again during business hours."

"Then he'll fire her and she'll kill herself. M and M Advertising, good morning."

"I'll get Garrick to take you down. Garrick!"

Garrick appears. Graying, fey, he bends—at the knees, at the waist, at the wrist—yet seems to move in agitation. His walk is a kind of complaint carried out in movement. "Don't scream at me. I've got six layouts to finish by tonight. Everybody around here thinks they can scream at Garrick."

He sulks as he dresses for his errand: a knee-length leather jacket and white silk scarf, too warm for the melting spring day, too decorative for the dust-balled elevator which is to take us downstairs amid sulking groans of its own.

Halfway down, the elevator shudders, then jams to a stop. I hold my breath. Garrick slams a fist against the wall. The elevator trembles and, persuaded, groans its way down again. Garrick is silent on our steaming walk to the restaurant. The streets are crammed with people of intense purpose, wearing summer-weight business suits, hailing cabs, filling the air with a restless drive. Garrick leaves me at the revolving door of the Palm. "Lots of luck," he says and trudges tragically back the way we'd come.

Inside the restaurant I blink blindly in the sudden dimness. The bar gleaming mahogany glamour, the mock-welcoming maître d'—it is all for a moment dazzling.

Then I get my first glimpse of Moss Gottlieb and Steinardt, the ruling gods of that first New York summer. Amid the fake sawdust and the waiters in butcher's aprons I find them lunching together, talking softly, hunched over the table in a curve of intimacy. When I approach they look up, startled, like illicit lovers caught in a tryst.

I know Moss Gottlieb from the picture in my father's college yearbook. The other is a husky chunk of a man, gray and grizzled with a beefsteak face. I'd never seen a man so closely shaven. An aura of too-sweet cologne and some sort of talcum powder surrounds him.

I stand at the table waiting to be noticed and welcomed. Moss greets me with the first of a million Gottlieb jokes designed to include you and to put you off at the same time. He glances up at me and says, "We've given our order, thanks."

The other man says, "Ah, this must be the promised racing maven."

For the third time that morning I say, "I'm Gordon Graff." It is beginning to sound like gibberish. Moss observes me over the glass in his hand. "Hello, Graff. Moss Gottlieb."

"Nee Moses," the other man says.

Moss carefully does not look at him or respond. "Sit down," he says. "Say hello to Nick Steinardt."

I do both and am rewarded with an unordered martini. In its flowering cup and long stem it is like an artifact found on another planet. I take a tiny, burning sip.

"I'm sorry I'm late," I say. "But nobody told me—"

Moss cuts this line of talk off quickly. "Graff is going to be your creative director on the project."

"Listen, Graff. Racing is at the heart of this project," Steinardt says. Each man invests the word "project" with a sacred sound. "I mean the world is not waiting for another credit card. But the racing can give it the push we need. We market the car and the driver—the card will tag along."

"I see," I say blindly.

Moss is watching me closely. He has a small, long face with a closely cropped black-and-gray beard. A few wisps of salt-and-pepper hair still cling to his head. His eyes move constantly; he puffs on his cigarette like punctuation in a sentence being written inside his head, a sentence only he can read.

"First time in the big city?" Moss says.

"That's right. I just finished graduate school in English. University of Virginia.."

5

"By God, a virgin,"

"I beg your pardon."

"Just an expression." He turns to Steinardt. "His father and I were roommates at Harvard."

Steinardt laughs. It is not a pleasant sound. "On the quota?" he said. "Graff . . ." Exaggerated comic pause. "Is that a Jewish name?"

"No sir. We're Catholics, but . . ."

"Catholics but, hah. A good WASC fallen among thieves." Steinardt grins. His smile has too many teeth. "Moss, here, is a WASH."

"I've never heard of that."

"A white Anglo-Saxon Hebrew."

"Don't start, Nick," Moss says. "Let the kid be a virgin, safe from the world's evil, at least till after lunch."

The arrival of food arrests some gathering of electricity in the air. Steinardt attacks a giant portion of roast beef, bleeding juice onto the sliced potatoes surrounding it. Moss picks at a chef's salad and sips another scotch barely invaded by water. I try the small steak. It must easily weigh two pounds.

"You're not eating, Moss." Steinardt seems to play different roles with Moss: goading client, now goading parent.

"I'm eating, I'm eating."

"You're paying," Steinardt says. "You may as well enjoy it." He invites me into the play. "This isn't Moss's kind of place. Too classy."

"Fake Americana," Moss mutters. "If I want butcher aprons I'll go to a butcher shop."

"Wait till he takes you to his favorite watering places, Graff. Moss has a taste for low-life unrivaled in the business. Patti Moore's, ask him to take you to Patti Moore's over on Third Avenue."

"Lay off Patti, Nick." Moss scowls. "She stood by me when things were bad. Which"—Moss raises his glass to toast the invisible stalwart friend—"is more than I can say for certain clients."

"At least this client is still here. Which is more than I can say for Scott Paper, Holland-America, Buick . . ."

"Do me a favor and stop singing the long sonata of the dead." He swivels to me, winks mysteriously.

It is like eavesdropping on a conversation in a foreign country. The syntax hints at a kind of war, yet the tone is easy, familiar; it speaks of ritual—exchanges repeated, in different forms, over and over again. Steinardt all bulk and aggressive presence, looming over the table; Moss fading after each duel, then a rally, a riposte, a sip of his drink and, again, a fade. The unaccustomed daytime alcohol blurs my reaction time. I observe and listen, confused, waiting for cues. I do, however, note that Moss has dispatched three scotches by the time the coffee arrives. They seem to make him by turns morose, then lively, then silent.

"How about an after-dinner liqueur, kid?" Steinardt asks.

"Not for me thanks."

"Moss?"

"Me? Jews don't drink." Moss's hand is already up for the waiter, ready for the snifter of brandy.

Dazed, I listen to them spell out the scenario for the marketing of a new bank credit card. It may have been the shock of arriving in the strangest of strange cities to me, New York, on the breathlessly unexpected hot day of April twentieth, nineteen-seventy-five; it may have been the difference between the Moss Gottlieb my father had prepared me for and the one I was seeing; it may have been the sense that I was a character in a masquerade I didn't understand, or it may have been the gently poisonous duel between Moss Gottlieb and Steinardt; whatever the cause, the Byzantine scenario has my head whirling.

". . . multimedia campaign . . . heavy on TV . . ."

"People think of credit as yielding, feminine . . . need a masculine image for the new card . . ."

"Racing car is the perfect symbol . . ."

". . . start with new name and logo . . ."

". . . everything builds to Indianapolis . . ."

". . . press conference . . . party after the race . . ."

". . . we're late already . . . How come we're always late, Moss?"

A newly expansive Moss turns to me, snifter in hand, veteran of unknown business wars ready to relate battle stories. He radiates warmth and charm, strokes his beard upward, then pulls at his mustache. It is the kind of mercurial change I would grow to expect, finally to dread.

"Would you believe, young Graff, that I've known this man—"

"This client!"

"This client for over twenty years and he has yet to be satisfied with what I've done for him."

"What have you done for me, Moss? Taken the account from a lousy two million six to ten million in billings."

"I love this man." He puts his arm on Steinardt's shoulder. I don't think he sees the man's stiffening under his touch. "That's what you've done for the agency," Moss says happily. "I'll tell you what we've done for you—as soon as I can think of it. But Graff here is going to help us do the biggest thing of all."

I hear the din of the place as if my ears have been magically cleared. The hardwood floor, bare but for a sprinkling of sawdust, absorbs nothing—gives back to the air a clamor of waiters' shouted orders, of customers' clanking cutlery, clinking glassware and dishes, the mutter of coups and campaigns. It is a terrorizing noise I've never heard before. Steinardt is standing. "Got to hit the head," he says. Suddenly he looms over me shedding the sickly sweet aftershave into the air. "What kind of heap did you drive at Daytona, Graff?"

"Drive . . . ?"

"In the race. When it happened—you know . . ."

"I promised the kid we wouldn't talk about it."

Steinardt sways subtly, like a mountain shifting on its geological base. I haven't counted his drinks as I have Moss's. He looks like a man accustomed to being in control of himself and others. "You guys," he says. He shakes his head gravely. "You always stick together, don't you." He marches with steady steps towards the bathroom.

Alone and safe, for the moment. Gottlieb's face collapses. "You're a trouper, kid."

"How do you mean—trouper?" I say with an edge I had no idea I could call on at this moment.

"I threw you a curve in there."

"Well, what is all this about me and racing?"

"Listen, he'll be back fast. He seems slow and deliberate—but he's fast. He even pisses fast. Just fake your way through. I'll cue you in later."

"But what was I supposed to have had . . . some kind of accident?"

"Play it by ear. Can't talk now."

But it is precisely talk which appears to be the real currency of this kind of place, not food. Talk, and the liquor and noise that make it possible to say dangerous things which cannot be said as safely behind a desk or in a conference room. There are so many questions tumbling over each other in my mind. What kind of people were "we"—that always stick together? Was Moss's first name actually Moses? And, if so, what was the joke in mentioning it the moment I arrived?

Steinardt might be fast but he was lingering in the john too long for Moss's comfort.

"Where the hell is he? Maybe he ducked out . . . saw through the Daytona stuff . . ." His expansiveness has shrunk to anxiety in seconds. He must have noticed my stare, read bewilderment for disapproval, and breaks out a smile for my sake.

"He did that to me once, Steinardt. Vanished and took the account with him. Just to scare me. A great practical joker: sadism masquerading as irony." As if on cue Steinardt reappears. "Just talking about you. The price you pay for going to the bathroom."

"Only human," Steinardt says, sliding into his seat and removing a mechanical pencil from his inside jacket pocket. He carefully turns up the lead point and begins to draw a diagram on the tablecloth.

"This is the checkpoint: We work back from that. Memorial Day weekend at Indianapolis."

"We can't make Indianapolis. That's only six weeks away. You've got lead time for four-color printing and we're shooting commercials on film not video, so there's color correction and lab time . . ."

"Maybe *you* can't make it. *I'm* going to make it with a big splash. If not with your marketing campaign then it'll be somebody else's."

"Of course we'll make Indianapolis! How do you think I got to be a corporal of industry! Gives us all of six weeks. Plenty of time." Moss winks at me to underscore his reversal. If he can make you smile, or even better, laugh at something, then it hadn't really happened. Steinardt gazes at him patiently. "We're putting three million behind this push. With two million backup for the second wave."

This calls for Moss to light up another cigarette. "Listen, we launched Amalgamated for half that in—"

"Don't sing that old song again, today. We've got a lot of work to do. Have you nailed down Wyatt?"

"Mickey's working on it."

"Mickey's working on his screenplay is what Mickey's doing. I want you to do it, Moss. Aren't you president of the agency?"

"Chairman. The switchboard girl is president. Okay, I hear you." A sobered Moss. "I'll have a contract by the end of the week." Aggrieved: "For Christ's sake, the guy's still on crutches from the spill in California. His wife said he was quitting racing. It's not simple. But we'll get him and we'll make Indianapolis even if we have to crawl there."

"That's the kind of talk I like to hear."

It is not the kind of talk I had expected to hear. Moss Gottlieb had been a poet of economics to my father. Moss had gone from Harvard to that world where the holders of power decided the financial destinies of the rest of us: the powers who launched new credit cards, or closed old, revered companies; those wizards familiar with the magic of a word that was to the late twentieth century what the word alchemy was to the twelfth century: marketing. Wizards of marketing who facilitated the giant mergers which caused a line of suddenly empty stores in the downtown section, and which Time magazine spoke of as "epochal" or "the passing of an era."

"Wild, he was a wild man," my father would say with worship in his voice. "Never studied—top grades; his practical jokes were genius, a kind of poetry." But like all poetry, Moss's practical jokes resisted translation. I had only my father's word for the unique Gottliebian qualities of verve and style they embodied. "He gave a comic lecture on Henry George's Single Tax Theory all in double-talk—had the class hysterical and at the same time laid out all of George's major ideas. He got an A. I would have flunked—or been thrown out."

The wild man is, for the moment, tamed. The tables around us have thinned out; waiters shake tablecloths and busboys lug silverware to the kitchen in wooden carriers. In the artificial twilight of dark wood panels and marble floors there is no hint that a bright spring afternoon waits outside to greet any survivors of the lunchtime wars.

A basic timetable has been set for the credit card launch but there are still, apparently, a few other details to be determined. Having seized the advantage—my untrained eyes may not have seen that he'd had it all along—Steinardt proceeds with more demands.

"I want one hundred percent of Graff, here, understood? I need racing know-how, not puffery."

A sullen Moss: ". . .'s why he's here, for Chrissake."

"And I don't want your airy-fairy Garrick for this push."

"Why not?"

"He's a print man This campaign's going to be heavy TV."

"We've got a new art director, Carl Morris the third—from the LA office of McCann. A great reel."

"The third? Jesus! Well, let me see his reel."

"I don't show clients reels of people I'm considering for the agency. We pick our own people."

"Are you looking for trouble, Moss?"

"Do I have to look far?"

"Why do you people always answer a question with a question? Listen, Graff—" Steinardt turns, unexpectedly, to me. "Here's who he's got over at Moss's Rolling Stones. For a copywriter he's got a young girl who's always on something and meditates half the day away in her office. He's got an old fag paste-up guy as an art director he keeps around because he's too cheap to hire real talent, he's got a partner who wears sunglasses in the office waiting for a call from the Coast on one of the screenplays he's always writing on my money, he's got a production department full of free-lancers who come and go depending on whether there's any money to pay them—and Maria, there's always Maria, who specializes in inventing original Renaissance Italian ways to meet payrolls and pay media bills. To this assortment of characters I am supposed to entrust a five-million-dollar launch of the most important new credit card idea in American banking. But I'm still not supposed to ask to see the art director's reel! Have you got all that, Graff?"

"Come on," Moss says with weary sarcasm, "enough of this fulsome praise. Surely you must have some criticism of your agency."

"Only one of my agencies, sonny boy. With the others all hungry for your share."

By addressing me directly, Steinardt has made me a player in the game, if only for a minute. I say, simply: "Then why do it?"

Steinardt turns his scowl into a broad, white grin.

"Good question. Because this man has been known to commit acts of creative marketing genius when sober."

Moss leans back in his chair and sips brandy. "I accept your apology," he says.

"Never mind. You'll accept my demands. Which are not finished."

"Hah!"

The duel continues.

Steinardt: "And no fancy dancing media barter for this one."

Moss: "You pay us cash, we'll pay them cash."

I had no idea who "them" was. I merely register that Moss is moving more and more to the defensive with each exchange. I am exhausted and can not take in much more information. I let their words slip by as if they are notes of music: abstract, embodying feelings, tone, nothing more specific.

". . . a launch party . . . racing world and the banking honchos, all the media," Steinardt is saying. "Personal favor . . . know what I mean, Moss . . . she may look like a madonna but I happen to know she's a very busy girl in the social department, anyway, and not always too particular. But she's damned pretty and she won't mind."

"Then you ask her."

"No, I want you to *tell* her."

Moss shakes his head, slowly, sadly. "Not in her job description."

"Then put it in her job description. You're so fond of telling everybody it's your agency."

"Is my agency."

"Then tell her she's my date. It's just for a party. Nothing heavy."

"You really thought I'd deliver her? Play the corporate pimp?"

"No thinking about it. I *know* you'll do it."

"Wanna bet?"

"Okay."

"For how much?"

Steinardt bends over the table and presses Moss's oval face between his two plump palms, like a father playing with his little boy.

"For everything," he says. "The account, your whole agency's lifeblood. The works. How's that for stakes? You're a witness, Graff." He holds my eyes with a fierce gaze, large, cool slits of ice blue taking me in, before I can waver. Then to Moss, "I'm going out of town for a week. Gives you time to think it over."

I say nothing, trying not to look at either one of them. I have no idea what this is all about but it feels ugly.

With the three of us en route to the exit, Steinardt says, "Excuse me," once again.

"There's no excuse for you," Moss says as his client makes his way, once more, towards the men's room. One weakness in the otherwise iron man seems to lie in his bladder. Moss, on the other hand, can absorb, camel-like, limitless quantities of alcoholic fluid.

We wait between the coat-check cubicle and the revolving door, next to the bar, Moss smoking and me watching him. He watches back, a narrow-eyed gaze.

"Do you realize," Moss says suddenly, "that within twenty blocks of here there are—maybe—say, seventy restaurants in which about three thousand people have lunch every day. But this exercise, this ballet of subtle and gross natives—what some poet once called the scrimmage of appetite—cannot be described and dismissed by an expression as mere as 'having lunch.' It's a romance of capital, a poetry of fiscal hungers fed by seduction and betrayal."

He is enjoying his role of Cicero with me as audience. This is, after all, the man who had slipped a parody lecture past a Harvard professor and won an A and my father's lifelong admiration.

"These people at their steaks, their pastas and martinis, are disposing of, and acquiring, the assets of the central industry of New York: the idea-manufacturing business. And what do they bring to this industry?" I recognize the oratorical device of the rhetorical question and am silent. "They bring," he presses on, "every deadly vice and virtue, eloquence and elegance, style; charming, seducing, threatening, lying, blackmailing, teasing with hope, destroying hope, proposing deals, raising rates, lowering expectations. Listen, you're a child of the provinces come to the capital city to seek his fortune— okay, so it's not the capital, what's the word I want—aha, the Imperial City, well if you could have heard the sounds all around you—three blocks north at the Four Seasons an editor who's terrified of losing his job makes an offer to an agent that's about fifty thousand dollars too high. But it brings the book in and by the time it comes out and bombs so badly it doesn't even scratch the surface of the advance, the editor's working at another house . . . and listen, two blocks east at Il Menestrello, an account executive okays a kickback from a printing supplier and gets drunker than usual from nervous guilt and at the next table the president of a TV production company tells his senior man that he's being retired because in two more years he'll be eligible for a fat pension—well, actually, he skips the last part but the guy knows what's being done to him . . . and a few blocks north at the Russian Tea Room a husband and wife team who run an ad agency are discussing divorce and the new account they've just brought in, with the same anxious high spilling back and forth from one to the other . . . Just a few tiny samples . . ."

Moss teeters before me, turning to the four points of the compass to illustrate his round-the-town Comedie Humaine of Lunch.

"You paint a grim picture," I say.

Grim but not without a certain loony eloquence. I can see for an instant beneath the balding, straggled-haired figure a hint of my father's household god: the laureate of buying and selling. He sways slightly and his blue eyes catch my gaze, an ironic slanted look. It is as if he knows what I am looking for; something, anything to ransom the sour aftertaste of this particular episode in the land of Lunch.

"Grim picture?" Moss is astounded. "It's goddamn thrilling. I love it all. I love them all. And I didn't dish up one fake example. I know every one. In fact George and Lucy, who owned Lester and Lowe, stayed on after the divorce—they almost bought M&M." He twists a grin at me. "A lot of potential buyers around. I could be living on the Riviera now. Hah!"

A rush of late-leavers envelops us.

"Hey, here's Mighty Moss."

"Moss the Magician."

The departing group is in disarray; three middle-aged men in business suits, one brown, two gray. The Brown's tie no longer quite meets his collar, the Dark Gray Suit has a spatter of red sauce on his white shirt, and Light Gray Suit is no longer precisely certain of how the simple act of walking is accomplished. They've had a convivial, extended lunch. This is long before the age of designer mineral waters with European names, when three martinis were still part of the job. It's hard to know if it was a more, or less, innocent time.

"Hey, Moss, what're you doing in these fancy digs?"

"Waiting for my client," Moss says. "Men's room. First Security Trust."

"Old Steinardt. We had that business, once. Let's have a drink at the bar while we're waiting."

Moss waves a hand loftily. "Never drink before sundown. Got a business to run."

Dark Blue Suit looks unconvinced.

All at once Moss remembers that I am there, a visitor from another planet.

"Gordon Graff," he said. "New creative director. From the South."

There follows a spill of names, of Jacks and Morleys, of J. Walters and Youngs and Rubicams and one man named Jerry-I-forget.

"C'mon Moss, just one more dose of medicine for the road."

The Brown Suit demurred. "I dunno; Moss gets pissed and funny things happen."

A stately Moss replied, "I never get pissed, merely slightly and pleasantly inebriated."

The Brown turned to the Dark Gray Suit. "Hah, as long as it's not like the time . . ."

"Yeah, the time he had to quit McCann . . ."

"Not quit—got canned . . ."

"And tried to stomp the Creative Director . . ."

"Not good on a resume . . ."

I don't know these people. Listening to them is like trying to do a crossword puzzle in a foreign language. Instead of listening I start worrying about what's holding Steinardt up. I want to leave, to get back to the Agency, to find a place to unpack my meager bags, to start what is supposed to be my real life for this enforced summer interlude. I am not savvy enough to understand that this *is* that life.

The events of the next ten minutes are like actions in a dream: there is the sense of cause and effect but they seem strangely disconnected. We move to the bar, mahogany still gleaming in the dim light but less enticing to me, now. The bartender seems to know everyone; even I am introduced; once again, Graff, the new creative director, whatever that is. Drink follows drink, martinis, whiskey sours, scotches, all with incredible swiftness, all interspersed with jokes, business jokes, dirty jokes, and all with—to me—obscure punch lines. They are speaking a code to which I do not have the key.

The last one is a long torturous joke I can not follow. Just before the mysterious punch line Moss falls against me with a deep sigh, eyes closed, chest rising and falling with a strange new rhythm. He emits a belch redolent of alcohol. As I struggle to keep him from falling, Steinardt returns at last. He seems to know everyone in the group.

He also seems to have complete knowledge of what is going on. This is apparently not a new, discrete event, but only another episode in a continuing story.

"Shit," Steinardt says, observing the almost comatose Moss. "I've seen this number once too often." At the sound of his master's voice Moss's eyes open. He starts to speak but Steinardt has gone through the revolving door, abrupt as a taste of vinegar. Moss stares after him, a twisted look on his face.

Gesturing towards the door he says, "You know the difference between the Yiddish and the British? The Yiddish say goodbye without leaving—and the British leave without saying goodbye." And having mustered his little remaining strength for that last riposte, he is only conscious enough to murmur, ". . . back . . . office . . ." He throws one arm over my shoulder and is gone to wherever it is the liquor has taken him; away from Steinardt, away from malodorous bets, from humiliation, away from consciousness.

Midtown Manhattan has been my island kingdom, now, for so many years that it's hard to see it as it was then to my twenty-three-year-old eyes; the sweep of bodies at noontime—the thrill of all that aggression in the sunny streets. But it seems to me that this particular New York I am picturing this afternoon—carrying a wounded warrior back from the battlefields of the Palm—is a city of embattled knights, where chariots, low-slung and belching fumes, wheel all around us, their insistent horns hailing some victory or defeat, it is hard to know which, pressing me on to some action, yet to be defined.

I lurch into the sun and shadow of 52nd Street carrying my sagging burden. That famous ragged skyline I'd seen only in movies cuts the sky with a heart-stopping beauty of line; the smell of gasoline and the sounds of car engines along the side streets make—foul acrid odors, raucous noise and all—that mixture of urban perfume and music that perhaps only the young find beautiful. I am young, I find it beautiful. It is all open, it is all promise.

We move south past the Citicorp Center, me leading an almost unconcious Moss Gottlieb back towards an office not on the storied Madison Avenue I'd come for, but one called Lexington. The crowded sidewalks throw every variety of humanity past us. As if to remind me of the subtle anti-Semitic undertones of the past few hours, a group of Jews wearing long black coats—in this heat—and skullcaps surround and then release us, speaking a variety of languages: Yiddish, Hebrew, and a garnish of what is probably Polish, Russian, and German. This is why I have come to New York. I, Gentile newborn that I am, thrust into my own personal diaspora.

As Moss and I stumble on our way, I realize my education has only just begun.

Apraxia

For Claire Feldman

S uch quiet! Especially there in the dark chambers of the night. He
has finished the evening's work, alone in the grand cavernous
living room of their country house. All the while he's sat on the long
beige couch, bought for one of the many new homes from which a
fresh start was to flower, listening to Shostakovich and writing two of
the pages with which he hopes to reverse the recent devastation of his
reputation, all this time Natalia has slept.

A giant black poster representing night is pasted against the
floor-to-ceiling window. A high hum of country silence has kept him
company while he worked. Inside the bedroom, behind a closed door,
Natalia sleeps her fragile, uncertain sleep.

Outside caterpillars silently suspend themselves from tree
boughs, from filthy beams in the garage, swinging right and left,
patiently waiting to be reborn as gypsy moths and devour every leaf
in the world. All else is suspended in silence and sleep. Suddenly—
click—the automatic timer on the window lamp switches on. It star-
tles him. The nerve of anxiety has been set in motion. It is time to go
to bed. In fact, a strange journey is about to begin.

He carefully removes the Shostakovich Tenth Quartet from the player and replaces it in its box. Old friend of the night written by a composer in terror of his life, old inner exile full of fears and song.

The record put to bed, what remains is the nightly tiptoeing blind man's odyssey around another's sleep. He undresses in the bathroom; clothes are left in a small huddle, a shapeless golem of his daytime self. Now he opens the bedroom door noiselessly: noise will wake Natalia, any noise, the slightest hint of movement carried on the air.

The dark room is a closed universe. Natalia has had shutters especially designed to keep out the wispiest ray of light. The dawn will come and go unnoticed and now not a finger of moonlight touches the interior of the bedroom. The darkness in the room is thick as tar. He pauses to let his eyes grow accustomed enough to the blackness to pick out shapes; he wishes to wait a second so as to hear her regular breathing, the seal of her safe sleep.

He moves a step; the floor creaks; swiftly he steps forward again, onto a rug whose location he knows perfectly. Then, lightly as a Schubert Impromptu, he turns the first corner, the corner of the bed, and stands, waiting. For what? For the memory that has come to him in the dark to become clearer: himself standing near another bed, his father's bed. In this memory it is also of the utmost importance that he not awaken his father. His goal is a chair near his father's desk, over which hangs a pair of gray trousers within which rest several twenty dollar bills, crumpled and careless so as to be unnoticed if gone, or so he prays as he gropes, steals, swift and silent.

His father slumbers on as does his wife, though in seriously different kinds of sleep. Memory is the other enemy besides sound; either can sabotage the trip to the bed. So far so good, the memory and the room are both quiet.

He listens, standing still, to her breath, before continuing. What sharpness of sound honed by anxiety. The country hum underlies all, but there is also a distant automobile horn and the sound of

"I mean, who is she?"

"She's your wife."

"I know, I know, not your mother, though." His eyes crinkle as if he is calling attention to some lewd joke they shared, "My second wife. Your mother and I—we were never, what's the word, compatible. But we knew each other. We knew who we were."

"Of course, Dad . . ."

"But at night, my second wife, she's a stranger. I go and stand in front of the bathroom."

"Why the bathroom?"

His father gazes at him with his wizened Trotsky-stare: a small, eternally rebellious man with a white goatee. "Because it's the middle of the night and I have to—you know, but I can't."

"Prostate trouble?"

"Ha—you call that trouble? It's the doorknob."

"What about it?"

"I don't know what about it. So I wake up in the morning and I'm asleep in front of the door and I'm wet through and through and how do you think I feel and how do you think your mother—I mean Lila—feels?"

A few days later in the doctor's office, he urges his father, "Tell Dr. Kroll." He tells the doctor, ending with an impassioned cry, "I don't know what anything's for at night. My wife, a doorknob."

"Yes," Dr. Kroll addresses his remarks more to the son than to the patient. "It's called apraxia."

"Ah," the son says.

"What?" the father says.

"From the Greek: praxis, practice, how to do things—it means unable, apraxia. It's nothing to worry about. It's a part of your brain that's not getting enough blood. So you don't recognize and remember what things are for—like turning the doorknob to open the bathroom door. I'm going to give you some pills . . ."

He remembers calming his still agitated father, pushing his skinny arms into jacket sleeves, trying to get the lining straight, while the old man murmured his fears. "It's all right, Dad. Everybody forgets. I forget." Little true lies that make him feel as if he were pushing twenty dollar bills back into those forty-year-old trousers—a theft restored. And, standing in the dark, he wonders if someday he may stand in some other distant dark wondering what doors are for, and beds, and who is that woman sleeping here?

But now he follows a thin ray of moonlight that has somehow evaded the shutter, to the edge of the bed and over Natalia's face. Hidden as she is, essentially unseeable in the night, he sees her as she was the first day they'd met, at the restaurant on 57th Street, elegant figure curved in a fashionable slouch, eyes reflecting intelligent sadness, an ironic, disappointed romance with hope which had recently ended—but darkly beautiful with possibility; sees her, too, years later, thickening into familiar love, knowing, funny, irritable, sensual. And as she'd been that very night before going to bed: sleepy, absently flirtatious, trailing nightgown, medicine, and magazine dreamily into bed; sees, in fact, the arc of their twenty years of life with each other—remembering how excited he'd been at their way of taking experience to each other, writing foolish reminders for himself: *tell N. about frog in sewer at 51st Street; tell N about remark Elliot Carter made about Hemingway and the Jews* . . .

In some way this encourages him—he will succeed in navigating this small voyage. He swivels on the toe of one foot and gives up all thoughts of failure. He's unreasonable on that subject, lately.

"It's too bad what happened," she said. "It was a fine book—told some real truths about music."

"What do you mean 'was'?"

"*Is* a fine book."

"Then why say 'was'? No eulogies, please."

"Did you know that the word eulogy has no grim connotations? It simply means praise."

"Tell it to the corpse."

No more of that. Turn to the immediate task. Only half of the voyage left. Is it half finished or half begun? One more step and the mathematical uncertainty will be resolved. Fifty-one percent means control in anyone's textbook. He steps; exquisite silence; steps again. A cricket comments dryly. Soon he will be lying on his side of the bed, blissfully asleep, all thoughts of failure buried in measured breath: he will be exactly as famous as the night.

But having interrupted his movement, how to start over? Starting again is, of course, the one essential problem. He's always done it. After Jemmy left, after Susan died, after Maurice quit, after his mother wasted with cancer, after his father turned out to be not entirely what he appeared, after Natalia developed a different idea about their marriage than his, after all these, he'd begun again.

Large and small losses: after losing his driver's license for the third time, after losing his erection for the first time and his publisher for the second time; after losing his job in Paris for the last time—after all these he'd begun again. If people died why not books, why not reputations? One could start again, apparently, after anything.

His father, the half-pint hero of old age, had started again at age eleven. Left behind in a Polish village by a fleeing father and a pursuing mother, he'd arrived on his parents' doorstep in New York to start over. Unfortunately, they'd already begun a new family and were not expecting his rendezvous with rebirth.

One foot in front of the other. Easy enough during the day, the sun approvingly guiding the way. But in the blackness, every floorboard threatening noisy betrayal, every ambiguous shape calling up some shade from the past, it was another matter. He'd thought it was his bedroom, his and Natalia's. But tonight it was so crowded! Once he got to his side of the bed and settled in they could be alone again.

But all at once the room is full of the dead: Jules in the corner, plump and morose; bouncy Alvin smashed up in a car wreck at nineteen standing near the door; elegant Martin, all British charm, his waning heart gradually draining him of breath, next to the window. He'd been asked to speak at all of their funerals, had done so with appropriate pain and inappropriate success. One thirty-year-old, pipe-clenched playwright saying afterwards, "Couldn't help thinking about that as a piece of writing while you spoke. Damned good." Himself dead two months later.

But worst of all was his beginning to write and rewrite, in his mind, eulogies for his friends before they died. It felt so good to chant praises, eloquently shaped—with carefully placed ironies calculated to draw little embarrassed laughs from an audience who came to mourn and were pleased by an unexpected smile. The premature eulogy; surely a better and safer form than the one he'd been practicing lately with such disappointing results.

Literary: "As Camus wrote in 'The Fall' . . ."

Colloquial/Raucous: "If there's anybody here Jack didn't lend money to, get up and leave, because you're a liar."

Ironic/Tender: "I never got a chance to tell Martin this, so it's now or never."

Burying your friends in your mind, before their time, all to feel—what? Prescient, apt, an appreciated writer if only in the theater of death. Shhh! She is turning in a rustle of bedclothes. The electric blanket clicks its mysterious Morse code. He wonders: when she goes to bed after him, as she sometime does, does she make a similar voyage? He assumes not; his sleep is not as delicate as hers. But he knows, too, the fragility of her sleep is not the issue. It merely provides the occasion, like an obsession for a writer, or a jewel box for a thief.

She'd owned a more reliable sleep, once. He remembers their on-again, off-again endless courtship. In those days she'd be asleep minutes after he dressed and was on his way, to pacify the puritan curiosity of the Irish elevator operator. She slept secure in her reputation and in her authentic innocence. It was all for love; not for sex and not for marriage—all for love. The sleep of the innocent, in truth.

Innocently, Natalia had introduced him to his subject: the Shostakovich quartets. She had been in the concert hall in Moscow as a child when the Borodin Quartet had played the Third; the composer was there, too, and she'd seen him bow. This was shortly before Stalin and Zhdanov clamped down hard on the composer, sending him back to personal terror and the writing of the later quartets in a kind of experimental autobiographical code.

"Why do you love these quartets so much?"

"Why did you give them to me?"

"Because I thought you'd love them."

"Well, I do."

"But—why?"

"Because they're beautiful."

"Just—beautiful?"

"In a certain way. He was imprisoned in his head, the quartets were like his prison diary. It was silent music, unperformed, so he could push himself to the edge of amazing song."

"Why did not being performed make his work more beautiful?"

"Censorship is the mother of metaphor."

"You didn't make that up."

"He was trapped—terrified of being killed—but he also couldn't not write the music."

Natalia closed her eyes under the string sounds. "I love them, too," she said. "I just wanted to know exactly what kind of heroism you admire. You'd better call your father," she reminded him, as she had every night since the old man started becoming an old man.

He would have liked to tell her that he admired her kind of heroism, as well. The way she'd taken her losses, which had been early and terrible. But he didn't, even though her eyes were closed and it would have been easier that way. You didn't talk to people you loved so easily about their losses. Unless they were Shostakovich, and then you waited till they were dead. When it was your wife's losses you waited for her to talk about them and you hoped you could hear about them without being wooden or sodden, since no one had invented an adequate response to the losses of people you loved, or of people you didn't love, for that matter.

The phone rings. He lunges for the bedside receiver before the second ring. To his ears it sounds as if a bomb has gone off. But a glance at Natalia's breast rising and falling with the same regularity speaks of the safety of continued sleep.

"Hello," he whispers, dragging the long cord as far as he can away from the bed and towards the window.

"Hokdskimd," someone says or something like it. Is it Swedish or Russian? He is used to some friends of Natalia calling and opening instantly into Russian, though never this late.

"What do you want? Who is this?" He sounds, to his own ears, like someone from an old horror movie, hoarse, perhaps a little mad. Serve them right for calling at this hour, interrupting his journey.

"Hello, Hoffmeister?" the voice says. He still cannot make out the nationality, as if it matters.

"No."

"Gregor?"

"No."

Hoffmeister and Gregor. So far, German and Russian. Why didn't he just hang up? Every word he spoke increased the chances of waking Natalia. It was as if someone had been watching his strange odyssey and had called to comment on it in a language he cannot understand. "Please," he says, "call back tomorrow. Don't call back tonight." Very gently he replaces the receiver.

He steps forward. A floorboard sounds the alarm, a loud, clear squeak. At the same instant a siren, somewhere in the quiet night, approaches the house. The phone call has set off a seismic series of sounds.

"Shto—shto etoy takoy . . . What is it?" Natalia is awake. Little remains of the two years she lived in Odessa before being brought to America, except an occasional midnight phrase startled from dreams.

"Nothing," he says. "I'm coming to bed."

"I haven't been able to sleep."

"Yes, you've been asleep."

"No, I've been lying here, trying."

"I heard you breathing—you were asleep. I'm sorry I woke you."

"Breathing isn't sleeping," she says. "I was wide awake."

"Go back to sleep," he says firmly, a hypnotist giving a command. Instantly she is silent and the steady rhythm of her breath is restored.

The awakening changes the nature of the journey. With swift, confident steps he rounds his side of the bed and slides beneath the blanket. He lies still for a moment, a destination achieved, process completed. But it does not somehow feel right; he's left with a sense of disappointment that Natalia was awake. Was she telling the truth about having been awake all the while he was stealthily voyaging around her? Impossible! It is important for him to believe his own story: she had slept, was briefly awakened, confused as to chronology of sleep and waking, and then had fallen asleep again at his command.

But what has been raised is the question of disappointment. He does not own the sensation. Natalia's disappointments lead their lives in the same night as his own. They are more mysterious, belonging as they do to someone else, but they exist and he knows or thinks he knows some of them by name. Work, children, death, money, marriage—disappointment was worked through them like a thread through fabric. But that was so true of everyone that it sounded a false note, even though true of her. Once she'd told him of an insight she'd had at about the age of seven—that nothing she looked forward to with great excitement and hope would ever satisfy, ever match those emotions. The downward curve was inevitable, built into the hope-system from the start.

The result of being hurtled from her home in Russia? Or an

inborn tendency to mistrust the rewards of experience? Too heavy for midnight questioning. Was either of them disappointed in being married to a disappointed person? And how much disappointment made you a disappointed person, rather than a man or woman with disappointments?

It is a disappointing train of thought; he gets off. He takes with him the sense that, unlike his father and mother, Natalia and he are compatible, their senses of hope and irony are not identical—but they fit, they complement each other.

He reaches for the round switch connected to the electric blanket—the room is country-cold—and pauses. For that icy second he has lost the sense of how to work the switch. It is a fraction of time and then he remembers and clicks the switch on. But it has happened and it makes his heart an urgent presence in his chest.

Apraxia! Apparently it was always lying in wait—a possibility. Not knowing how or why to use things; how different was that from not knowing what to make of things—a common enough condition. It was all a matter of mathematics, his worst subject. Multiply confusion enough and you reached—apraxia. Nevertheless, the blanket is working its magic. Warmth creeps up the bed towards his stomach, his heart, his brain. Who knows, he may soon be warmed into sleep.

As he is dozing into darkness, he hears a voice, a man's voice, intoning a eulogy, his own. He cannot make out the words and wonders which of his friends is performing a premature elegy for him. His wondering is without anxiety, calmed by his half-sleep. As in a dream he is aware of the subject being discussed without having to hear the precise words. The subject is, of course, himself, but the tone is gaily lyric. This is no language of the grave.

The grave, he realizes, is the true home of apraxia: the place where there is no use for anything. No doorknobs, no bathrooms, no nights or days, no wives or husbands or fathers or mothers. But imagine, the voice is saying, imagine a kind of divine, benign apraxia, while one is still alive. Only think—not to know exactly what people are for; to reach out to them each time as if for the first time, unmuddied by categories, open, disinterested, without specific use or value. To know, in other words, the difference between a person and a doorknob; to be an idiot-savant of love reaching out with a simple, perfect touch. What an elegant defense against the barrage of disappointments which informed so many of the lives he knew, including on occasion, his own.

He is so taken by this idea that he wants to turn to Natalia and tell her, right then. Instead he falls into his own sleep at last, the beat of his breath joining hers in the darkness.

In the middle of the night, hours later, he wakes, his bladder pressing urgently downwards. He stumbles out of bed, now careless of Natalia's sleep, clumping noisily against the side of the bed. In front of the bathroom door, feeling for the doorknob, he stands, struck still by the connectedness of all things—recalling his mother and his father, at the end, lying in their comas in different years, in different hospitals—breathing in and out, unwakeable, the softly hissing bellows of his life—compatible at last.

Foxx Hunting

Could there be anything more humiliating, more ridiculous, than falling hopelessly in love, in middle age, with a porn actress seen only on video? Well, that's what happened to Schellinger. And not even a star; a second-rank young woman whose billing was "and Sarah Foxx." Schellinger had been struck by the plain honesty of the name Sarah when the other women all called themselves Brandy or Desiree, some simplicity in this strange new world.

Of course, Schellinger was no stranger to humiliation: an unexpected widower, a sales manager for an electronics company, parts not systems, suddenly forced into early retirement. This last had not come out of the blue—the company had been acquired and shakeups were in the air—but to Schellinger it had seemed to come with a painful swiftness and a cold substituting of numbers for human concerns.

He'd always been an odd duck in that world of wholesale and retail sales, as helplessly in love with music as he now was with the will-of-the-wisp, small-screen Sarah Foxx; especially, for some reason no one could explain, least of all Schellinger, in love with the soft impressions of the French music of the late nineteenth and early twentieth century: Debussy, Ravel, Satie, Poulenc—even that oddest duck of all, Reynaldo Hahn, who, record liner notes had informed him, had been a lover of Proust. Other musical loves included Faure, even smallish figures like Vincent D'Indy.

He'd majored in English and minored in musicology at Columbia and none of his friends could believe it when he abandoned musicology for a job with Phoenix Electronics. It started with a job demonstrating sound equipment, thus he could use samples of the music he loved; but that was small potatoes, a dead end, and he moved up into component sales. Finally parts beckoned and sales was his destiny. Where would musicology have led? He could have taught maybe, if he could afford to get a Ph.D. which he couldn't. Overeducated for any life he might carve out, he was surprised himself when he got involved in electronic parts, condemned to the banalities of the marketplace—even more surprised when he asked Nora to marry him, at a concert intermission, after she'd told him she didn't much care for the Ravel Piano Concerto.

"You mean you didn't like the performance?"

"No, it's the music. Too—I don't know—vague, fuzzy."

Schellinger was a master at surprising himself, unpleasantly. With himself for a friend he didn't need enemies, and his musical love had been a lonely sort of passion, an isolated life, with never a soul at work he could talk to about such things. He'd lived like a masquerader, faking his way through Monday morning quarterbacking coffee klatches about this end run or that home run before comparing this quarter's sales figures for this or that territory; and all the while Schellinger would be secretly full of the thrilling Sunday discovery of a Maggie Teyte recording of Berlioz's *Nuits de'Été* in a musty shop on Park Avenue South.

Schellinger and his wife had been reasonably happy, though they both knew that he was a difficult man to whom ordinary pleasure came hard. He'd once replied to a friend who'd asked if he'd had a good time on a European vacation, "You have to understand, having a good time is not my idea of a good time." But when forced out of his job, with just about enough retirement money to get by—if he went easy on the summer music festival trips to France—that was when Schellinger mourned with a ferocious anger. Nora had been a quiet, gifted woman, a choral singer who gave private voice lessons at home; they'd had no luck having a child of their own and had raised her daughter by a previous marriage. He and Nora had grown quite close, finally, Nora always after him to go back to college, get his Ph.D. in musicology. When he moaned and groaned about the difficulty, she kidded him about his "anhedonia," his inability to organize happiness, joy in his life. It was as if some sort of irony had become his way of getting through the day. If you couldn't have what you wanted, or worse, didn't know quite what you wanted, then you detached yourself from wanting. He was not the first frustrated man to decide that desire was a game for fools. Only their vacations seemed worthy: a trip to Provence, reading Ford Madox Ford, a trip to Cyprus, reading Lawrence Durrell; vacations and weekend record-hunting excursions.

Nora registered only the mildest of happinesses, herself. Still, the only real complaint he'd had about her was her smiles, the lack thereof. She owned a full-scale laugh, could bellow it forth when amused. But day-to-day, Nora lacked the urge, or the ability, to smile. It was not something you could request of a woman: "Could you smile, please, from time to time, so that the air will seem brighter, a sense of possible joy in the universe, not to mention around the house."

Smiles had always been inordinately important to Schellinger. Perhaps because genuine pleasure was such a stranger to him, he needed the outward simulation of joy, goodwill, the sign of being pleased, whatever smiles meant. Jill, the girl before Nora, had accused him of wanting smiles mainly from women. "You don't give a flying fuck if men smile at you; it's some kind of giving in you need from women, some proof that whatever woman you're with is pleased—to be with you, at what you're doing, at what you've just said, just at your existence in the world. For Christ's sake, you get upset if a woman on TV doesn't smile after a while."

Jill didn't last long, replaced by Nora, the question of smiling covered by her outrageous laugh. Happy or not, to be suddenly deprived of his wife of twenty-eight years and then rejected by his company of twenty-two years, this was enough to ignite a fifty-year rage: so went the arithmetic of Schellinger's miserable anger.

It was in this mood that, lonely, at loose ends in the day and at night, he began his adventure with pornographic videos. At first it was desultory, a mild peeping into imaginary sexual lives with real people; fairy tales of endless virility and infinitely passionate, eager women. He even allowed himself the luxury of masturbating a few times, something he'd not done for years, afterwards feeling not so much shame as self-pity: left alone and forced to this, that kind of feeling.

He was not yet ready to be with a flesh-and-blood woman; a few disastrous blind dates, one arranged by his brother-in-law and one by an ex-business associate, had demonstrated that. Both had been feasts of awkwardness, and neither woman had ever heard of Debussy. So he retreated to the videos, drawn by the presence, on one, of a dark-haired, plump-cheeked beauty who went about her activities with an odd kind of half-smile and an enthusiasm which seemed—childish idea—entirely genuine. Schellinger was not naive enough to believe that these exercises in fantasy were in the smallest way real: all the multiple coupling, the mouthing, the thrusting, the moaning, the twisting, the spurting, these were a shadow play, a distant echo of anything real. Nevertheless, this one young woman who entered into all these activities with a kind of zest all her own, the ever-present half-smile resting on her sweet mouth in between the obscene uses of that sweet mouth, moved him in some odd way, soothed his lonely rage. It was the smile, in the midst of all that carnage, that got to him.

But after the first film, Schellinger could not find any more films in which she appeared. There were lots of other Foxxes; the name with its double-x symbolism was a favorite in the sex-symbol-ridden porn universe: also men with names like Johnny Wadd, T. T. Bone, women called Heather Foxx and Little Annie Sprinkle. All this scholarship came from browsing, but it did not produce the Sarah he was in search of.

In desperation he struck up a conversation with the blue-cheeked manager of one of the stores. Irritated at being distracted from the task of cooling a cardboard container of coffee while checking a string of figures, the guy gave him a quick brushoff. Schellinger figured he must be used to a lot of weirdos asking questions. "Nah," he told Schellinger, "they don't list them by actresses. You just gotta look. Try the catalogue."

There was, then, a catalogue. Schellinger would have preferred porn videos to exist in an uncatalogued, subterranean never-never land. A catalogue gave a kind of businesslike legitimacy, removed it from its aura of the forbidden. It conferred an order on this underground world.

Underground or not, apparently Sarah Foxx was not an important part of it. She was not to be found in the catalogue and she was returned, for the moment, to the refuge of Schellinger's imagination. Had she been a college girl who'd blundered into pornographic films to make the tuition her family could not afford and then quickly quit? Daughter of a blue-collar family, perhaps in West Virginia or some other appropriately poor, strictly religious environment?

He worried, too about AIDS, and tried to find out the exact year when the Foxx film was made. If it was made in the seventies when both she and Schellinger would have been in their twenties, then he could breathe a little easier. It would be impossible to enjoy the easy sensuality of their imaginary relationship if he had to worry about her health.

It was, in its way, as real as his relationship with his lost but well-remembered Nora. He had a videotape he'd made of Nora at a birthday party when she'd laughed so hard at a joke someone else had told that she could not stop and her joy seemed almost like pain. But still it was laughter and pleasure and he played it now and then, though perhaps not as often as the one video of Sarah Foxx that he'd been able to buy, the only one, he now suspected, that she'd made.

He noted that she wore only a teddy in the film, at least to start with, and he tried to assign some significance to this. A sense of classic style as in Victoria's Secret catalogues? Delicacy? An old-fashioned-ness—as if these porn flicks were home movies in which she could express her own tastes and sensibility via wardrobe?

In an attempt to get to know her better, visually, Schellinger took to freeze-framing to get her in close, but it was always wrong: too much on the side, her breasts visible but her expression hidden, her long, lovely legs curved around some man but her half-smile out of the frame. He wanted to see her sexual activity at the same time as her soul shining out of her long-lashed wide eyes. It seemed to him that there was something soulful about the way she paid her caresses, the way she made herself available, the smile that preceded each intimacy, a kind of detached good humor, as if to say: okay, we're here in this crazy situation. Since genuine passion is ridiculous here and now, let's do what we have to do with energy, goodwill, and a little irony. I'm young, I like sex, and if this is only a parody, well, what the hell, parodies can be enjoyed, too. Schellinger carefully avoided the other inevitable interpretation: that this was a degrading of women, a manipulation by men, commerce, prostitution, the use for money of something that was meant to be given, not traded in, ever. He was after his own fairy tale, in no shape, yet, to handle reality.

In any case, getting close to the spirit and image of Sarah Foxx by freeze-framing was an impossible idea. It turned out unsatisfactorily each time. When you freeze-framed on a video, a long, black, shimmering band of interference covered the center of the picture. Hopeless to search for clarity under these circumstances. Foolishly in love with a screen image, Schellinger was at the mercy of cameramen, of directors—did they have real directors, were there Francis Ford Coppolas, Hitchcocks of orgiastic scenes? He had no idea; what he had was an obsession and no way to get any closer to it.

He was about to watch, one night after a dinner of leftover cold spaghetti, when he realized he'd put in the wrong tape: he was getting a blur of evening news and part of a TV movie. Schellinger hit eject and stared at the tape with ice in his nerves. It was the right tape: he must have recorded over it; he was given to taping shows, using the same tapes over and over. In despair he ran every second of the tape but there was not a trace of the original left.

In the middle of that night, sleepless with anger at his own stupidity, it suddenly came to him: if you didn't have the filmed woman anymore, find the woman herself. She'd be older, of course, but she looked to be only in her early twenties at the time. Since he had no idea when the video had been made, the year, age, all of this was uncertain. But the trick was: find Sarah Foxx in the flesh.

The next morning, in his desperation, he did something thousands of men have done when they wanted to find a woman they loved who had slept with other men: he searched out a private detective.

Sitting in the waiting room of John McGuire, Licensed Private Investigator, two floors above 32nd Street he felt once again involved in parody. Was everyone who sat on this stale-green couch, gazing at the rug with a round worn spot in the center, pursued by images from movies, television, novels? Was there no way to start fresh, to be one's self?

John McGuire, at least, was himself: freshly pressed gray slacks, blue blazer, striped tie, a preppy remedy for all private-eye cliches.

"This Sarah, she's your daughter?" McGuire seemed actually concerned, perhaps a father himself.

"No," Schellinger said.

McGuire's expression changed, his mouth drooped a bit—in dis-appointment, scorn? "Aha," he said softly. "A girlfriend? Wife?"

"I've never met her. Can't you just take the assignment of finding her without knowing why?"

McGuire frowned, considered the question as if it had a difficult intellectual dimension. "Everything helps," he said. "Like a jigsaw puzzle. You need every piece before you can put it all together."

Schellinger was apprehensive; the signs were not good for suc-cess. "I don't want to make it harder than necessary. But I have absolutely no relationship to this young woman. Zero."

McGuire stood, like a prospective employer who had interviewed Schellinger, learned all he could, and had decided the interview was over. He would give it his best shot, he told Schellinger. He would not take forever; he understood that Schellinger was a man of limited means.

Forever turned out to be six days. Like the Lord, McGuire knew how to work on a limited time budget. Over a cappuccino on Third Avenue he gave Schellinger his report. "She's living in Los Angeles," he said. "That's where the film was made." McGuire handed him a folder. "Her name is Everard. All the data's there, address, phone number." He smiled in appreciation of his own craft. "I thought this would be the toughest missing person assignment I ever had. I mean she wasn't even missing, just—absent from real life, living on the screen."

"Then how—?"

"It turns out this porn world is very small, maybe a hundred, two hundred people in it. I checked on the Internet, lucked into Al Guthrie, the guy who'd produced *Private Secretary*. He's out of the business now. Remembered her—an unusual girl, he said."

Schellinger was smelling triumph now. "Unusual, how?"

McGuire polished off his cup, delicately wiped a cappucino moustache from his upper lip, and waited while Schellinger wrote out a check for six days plus expenses: seven hundred and eighty dollars even. It would put him into checking overdraft but he was happy to write it.

"He didn't say in what way unusual," McGuire told him.

But Schellinger didn't care. His breath was caught high in his throat, thrilled at the prospect of finding Sarah Foxx, thrilled and terrified.

During the landing at LAX Schellinger found that the thrill was gone, leaving only the terror. First there was the fact that he had hardly ever traveled beyond the East Coast. And what the hell was he doing chasing an image of a girl, a woman now, to Los Angeles? What was he going to tell her? Or ask her? Would she call the police? Worse, would she laugh at him, some voyeur pervert chasing cross country to find his dream girl? He had an introductory plan, a cover story that he hoped would at least gain him entrance, a conversation. After that he hadn't the fuzziest idea of what to expect from the encounter. Nothing sexual, his obsession wasn't that crazy. He couldn't answer or even formulate his own questions, could only hope that, when the moment came, she would, by her existence, in the flesh, clarify everything.

He'd planned his arrival for a Sunday, to catch her at home; had called and hung up after hearing a woman's "hello?" The fact of his surprise at the upscale street on which she lived—houses with long lawns, gabled facades—gave him an unpleasant hint: he'd been primed to feel sorry for her. This gave Schellinger a brief wave of disgust at what unpleasant, secret engines might be driving his trip. In front of Sarah Foxx's house a young boy of about nine or ten was attacking the bark of a tree with a pocketknife: her son, perhaps? This was hopeless, Schellinger was just stalling.

She was radiant: whatever he had responded to in the film, that mysterious half-smile, the plump dark curve of her cheek, the calm sensual confidence, the flowing black hair glinting with hidden lights, her seductive mouth which was like a mouth in a lipstick ad, it was all still there; but it was as if someone had taken that lissome young girl with her transcendent energy and turned her over to a Hollywood makeup artist who'd given her the sheen of fifteen or twenty years, a sophistication and poise along with a thickening at the waist and a few lines of fatigue around the wide brown eyes.

Her smile was cautious, barely stretching the corners of her mouth, tentative, the smile you offered a salesman or a Jehovah's Witness. Nevertheless, it called up memories, confirmed identity, validated his journey.

"Hello, Miss Everard," he said.

"Mrs.," she said. "And—?"

Standing in the doorway, he unleashed the cover story he'd planned out on the plane. He was a Professor Kalichstein at Columbia University—he'd stolen the name from one of his favorite pianists—and was doing a study on the explicit films of earlier generations, interviewing actresses, directors, distributors. (Why not go back to college and get his graduate degree in a masquerade, try it on for size late in life. Nora would have liked that.)

She interrupted, blowing it all away with a sigh. "I knew somebody would dig it up sooner or later," she said. "Shit," she said.

"Come in." She led him into the house, resigned, a prisoner on the lam who'd built a new life, facing the pursuing law at last.

Seated in the kitchen, with coffee and cinnamon smells in the air, she gazed at him across the table. "So," she said, "I guess Larry sent you."

"Larry?"

"No games, please. We've been divorced for years. But I know what he's up to."

"No such thing—"

She set down coffee mugs in front of each of them without asking if he wanted any. Pouring, she said, "Listen, being in a porno-film may not be nice, but blackmail is a serious crime. You tell that to Larry Everard."

Schellinger, heart pounding, simulated innocence by sipping the coffee, black, though he usually took sweet and low and skim milk. All he could think about was how to get out of this out-of-control mess. He took a deep breath and stood up. Do it fast, he thought, no talk, just get out.

"Sorry," he mumbled. "Misunderstanding . . ." He turned out of the kitchen, heading for the front door, keeping his eyes straight ahead, waiting for her to scream anger at him. He heard only her footsteps, first walking after him then running, and then her head was rammed into his spine and he was tumbling to the floor face down, her knee squeezing pain into the small of his back; he thought he could feel blood oozing from his nose where it had struck the hardwood floor; when she breathed words into his ear he smelled cinnamon on her breath.

"Listen, you son-of-a-bitch, you tell me exactly why you're here—now!"

God, he thought, what could he tell her? She would keep him lying on the floor forever, his nose bleeding over his jacket, his shirt, her small throw rug, everything. Who'd have thought he'd have

Sarah Foxx on top of him, three hours after arriving in L.A.? Schellinger started to laugh but laughter needed air and Sarah Foxx's knee was in charge of his air. It felt as if he'd been lying there for hours, his gaze filled by the bottom of an umbrella stand decorated with falling cats and dogs. Why, he wondered, an umbrella stand in Los Angeles where it never rained, least of all cats and dogs. But he didn't really care. He could happily lie under her, bleeding away, for hours, maybe days. Because, as quickly as cats and dogs, Schellinger knew the answer to her question—why he had come all this way to find her. He knew, now, exactly what it was he wanted from his crazy quest. It was the simplest thing in the world. He'd just wanted to be with Sarah Foxx; to see if being with her would help him understand the image of the young Sarah that had so attracted and haunted him.

"Okay," Schellinger said. "Okay, lemme up."

"Not until—"

"Hey, I'm bleeding."

They sat, again, in the kitchen while she scurried around getting an ice pack, apologizing for the coffee being cold, having too much cinnamon. With his head back, his tie opened at the collar, the chill spreading through his teeth and head, Schellinger told her the truth: the long old truth of Nora's death, of his being kicked into retirement, of his discovery of her film, her video, a life-saving obsession for him; then he told her the short truth: the truth felt face-down, bleeding on the throw rug, his vision of her, disrobing, mounting and dismounting, being mounted and dismounted, playing at being the horse or the rider with equal gusto, as if everything was her own idea, as if she had magically appeared inside this tacky universe of fake/real sex, like a real person full of quirks and nerve arriving in a bad novel crammed with cardboard characters playing at mechanical sex, letting herself be used with good-humored gusto but refusing to be degraded—a hero of her own life. How did she do it? How had she actually done it? How would she have behaved at his Monday morning sales meetings, week after soul-mashing week?

She stood before him, shaking her head, the half-smile of decades ago on her lips, right on the button. "That is," she said, "such a *farkakte* story, it has to be at least a little true."

Her face was flushed from exertion, those lovely rounded cheeks pink and brown, merged into a dark overlay. Her new friendliness was such that Schellinger actually thought she might apologize but that was not in the cards. Instead she came around behind him, seized his head and bent it backwards, pressing the ice against some magical pressure point of his nose. The bleeding was over and it was time for coffee and confession, this time from Sarah Foxx, Everard, whoever she was, moving them into the living room with their Provençal-designed coffee mugs.

"First of all," she said, "my name was Fuchs, Sarah Fuchs, not Foxx, it was never Foxx. Nobody used their real names, especially in those days."

"I guessed," Schellinger said. "All those Foxxes with one or two x's. There was even one with three. Did you know her?"

"I didn't know anybody," she said. "Do you want some more coffee?"

He sipped and asked, "What do you mean you didn't know any-body?"

"I only made the one. Then I was out of there, there being Los Angeles."

"And why all these foxes? Is that some kind of code?"

She gazed at Schellinger like a child at the zoo, curiosity, fascination. Innocent Male: North American Variety. "Foxy just means sexy. A sexy girl is a fox. Don't you ever watch TV?"

By the third cup they were like old friends, mistaken identity, tackling and bloody noses all behind them; a first date, then I did this, then I did that, information being exchanged, intentions still unclear. Schellinger had to pee, unused to so much coffee at once, but he didn't want to break the thin thread of unexpected ease spinning out between them.

He asked her, "Why the umbrella stand in the foyer, with the cats and dogs? It doesn't rain so much in L.A., does it?"

"I lived in Seattle for a time," she said. "I was happy there, so I brought it here for good luck."

"Did it work?"

"Not till you showed up, today." She grinned, more like a kid than a flirting grown-up woman. "You distracted me from my tzures."

"Your—?"

"Troubles. It's Yiddish."

She perched next to him on the couch, knees folded under her. She was wearing a skirt and blouse, the skirt navy blue, the blouse white, no adornments, a schoolgirl effect. Schellinger traced the curve of her throat down to the rounded shape of her breasts, remembering Sarah Foxx wearing only a teddy, trying to remember how she'd looked entwined with those men, her breasts a focus of their hands and mouths; but it was growing vague, now, impossible to compete with the living, older woman with her energy, her physical attacks, her Yiddish words.

On the way to the bathroom, the trip now unavoidable, he passed a bedroom, an unmade bed, with sheets and blankets turned down on one side. On the bed lay a flute and some sheet music—a piece Schellinger has always loved, for flute, unaccompanied, by Debussy, could it be the one? He was tempted to take a closer look but other urgencies called. He splashed his face with cold water; perhaps it would make the entire trip, the present moment, less hallucinatory. When he returned to the living room she was gone.

Schellinger sat on the edge of the couch. He took a sip of cold coffee and then she was back carrying something folded in tissue paper and a video cassette. "All the years I was raising Larry's kids I used to keep these in a bank vault. I didn't want them to stumble on them, but I didn't want to throw them away, either. I was lucky—he had girls. Still, I used to have a few nightmares about some guy showing them *Private Secretary*." She blinked quickly about a dozen times. "I don't know—I never saw a copy anywhere, after the first year. I don't know how come you found yours." She grimaced, a squinting of her eyes, on the verge of laughter, and tossed both items onto the couch. "My mementos of adolescent rebellion."

"How old were you?"

"It was in the spring of '71. I was twenty. But I was an adolescent, trust me."

He wanted to tell her about his anxieties, his concern about her health, AIDS, venereal disease. But 1971 was probably before AIDS, and she only did the one film, after all. Not wanting to be patronizing, inappropriate, he said nothing.

She unfolded the package and out came a teddy, mothballs spilling onto the living room floor. That familiar beige teddy, lace-trimmed, almost Victorian, setting her apart from the other women in the amateurish sketch portions of the film: Schellinger couldn't believe it existed in the real world.

"Of all the people I know—or don't know—in the world, you're the only one who's come back to me about all this." She held the teddy against her middle. "God, I wonder if I could still fit into this little jobby."

It had become something of a game for Sarah. From paranoid rage to a lark down memory lane. Schellinger was finding it hard to keep up with her.

As if to prove she was not out of surprises yet, she said, "Do you know what I did, about three years after making that video—since you're so interested—I wrote a check for the exact amount Al

Guthrie paid me, seventeen hundred bucks, and I sent it to the United Jewish Appeal—this was right after the Six Day War and they could use it. I wanted the slate clean. I didn't want to ever stay paid for that." She shrugged, sipped coffee and grinned with mischief. "I could even pay somebody—well, maybe. But not the other way around."

"I don't know why, but it never occurred to me that you might have done it for the money. Something about your smile."

She lay back on the couch looking past him, the teddy spread against her middle. Ignoring his gaze and following her own, she offered him the young Sarah Fuchs, midtown child, only child of Dr. Aaron Fuchs, psychiatrist, and Lena Fuchs, research consultant to liberal political action groups, waking her early on Saturday mornings to join them in demonstrations, march up Fifth Avenue, March on Washington, America Get Out of Vietnam, Doctors Against Nuclear Testing. By the time she is a sophomore at Columbia she is ripe for her own rebellion.

"As soon as I met Al Guthrie at this party I knew I would do it."

"Why?"

"I guess to separate myself from Aaron and Lena. I was stuck to them like glue."

He laughed. "You picked some way."

"Only in my head. They never found out. My plan was to let them find out, see it, whatever, hope that somebody would tell them." The giggle made her a young girl again, for the moment. "I lost my nerve. And the gods must have been looking out for me. The whole thing vanished. I got married to Larry Everard after college and I raised his two girls. I was thankful they were girls, but then I used to be scared some boy would discover it and show it to one of them. But—never."

"And nobody ever made trouble for you about the video?"

She pointed a finger at Schellinger, then stood, trailing the silken teddy behind her. "Only you."

"I'm not here for trouble. Anyway, not yours—just mine."

Her face darkened, eyes squeezed in a new mask. "Listen, that was all bullshit," she said.

Schellinger was startled. Was she turning against him again?

"What—about my trouble?"

She was not listening, intent on settling something of her own. "It wasn't my folks, their hearts were too much in the right place but they were fine. It was fucking Al Guthrie. I was hooked on him from the word go. Smooth, sweet-talking Al—I was like some fourteen-year-old high school kid just-hatched from Minnesota with her beloved pimp—'Do just this one for me, honey. I need this, just once for me . . .'" Her lipstick ad of a mouth curved down in disgust.

She tossed the teddy down next to Schellinger. "What's your real name?" she said. "I'm telling you the story of my life and you've probably come a dozen times watching me, don't you think I should know your name?" He told her and she flopped down next to him, as if exhausted by this new information, exhausted by her sudden storm of anger at the young Sarah Foxx nee Fuchs. "God," she said, "all that heavy money for Brearly, for the Ethical Culture School, all down the drain so I could tie up with Al Guthrie because he wore a red bandanna around his forehead and thought bourgeois life was garbage; just so I could make a fuck-flick and stick my tongue out at the world, just so he would love me when he couldn't love anything but his own dumb self." For a moment she closed her eyes and breathed softly, imitating rest. Then, a swift jump up to the stereo in the corner of the living room and the tender sound of a flute accompanied by strings infected the air: Vivaldi. Schellinger started in the nineteenth century; he was not crazy about Baroque music.

"Need some music therapy; I've learned to take some of the hard edge off," Sarah said. "That's Marcel Moise, the best."

Schellinger knew the name, had, indeed, a recording of Moise playing his favorite, Debussy's "Syrinx." Sarah sat down next to him and played out another recording, the coda to the story of her video:

how she returned to college, got her degree, married a nasty, middle-class version of Al Guthrie, Larry Everard, avant-garde playwright, divorced him, married a gentle physicist, years younger than she, moved with him, first to Seattle, then to UCLA. He died eight months later. The son-of-a-bitch Everard never gave up trying to get her back in his life.

"So you thought your first husband sent me," Schellinger said.

"Never mind—I don't think about him much anymore. I do my secret passion these days."

Schellinger said, "Your passions seem right out where you can see. That's what's wonderful about you."

She gave him a look of perfect scorn. "You think you know me because you saw me doing all that stuff with those guys. Mistake. I know you better from what you poured out at me over the first coffee cup." Schellinger's heart gave a jump; not a thrill, a jump of fear. She didn't sound so happy about what she'd heard—Schellinger's vision of this woman, so in command of her soul that she could swim in any dirty waters and stay clean—maybe clean him up, as well.

"I always wanted to play the goddam flute and Larry just laughed at me. It helped me get up the nerve to throw him out—well, to get out, myself, finally. Now my secret passion is in the open. Want to hear me play?"

It was not a question. She grabbed his hand and pulled him up off the couch, along the foyer and into the bedroom, where he had first glimpsed the flute lying in wait for its moment. There were details which had been invisible, earlier: a blue pair of pajamas near Sarah's pillow, a book, *Poems by*—the author's name was hidden by the thrown-down corner of a bedsheet. Schellinger was in deep waters but he was excited at this unexpected turn. Sarah picked up the flute.

Breathless, Schellinger asked, "Do you know 'Syrinx'?"

"What's that?"

" 'Syrinx,' a piece for solo flute. It's by Debussy?"

Scorn, which seemed to be Sarah's natural mode, reappeared. "Debussy?" She held her flute in one hand, a weapon. "That French impressionism stuff? Don't tell me you like all that. It's ear soup."

Schellinger was dead silent. She couldn't know how he felt about Debussy and all his French companions, but he took a tumble inside anyway.

"Listen to this," she said. "Gluck. *Orpheus and Eurydice.*"

Behind them, from the living room, Marcel Moise was still evoking the squares and rectangles of Vivaldi; now Sarah raised her flute in that exquisite gesture of holding a silver rod at arm's length while blowing the most intimate of breaths into its own mouth. First she turned off the vestige of her smile, peered solemnly down at the music; the looser-spun line of Gluck and the geometry of Vivaldi mixed in the bedroom air. He tried to remember, was Gluck Baroque too, but that stuff was all so long ago. Earlier, maybe, but it was beautiful and terribly, terribly sad in its long slow melody, mourning-as-wanting, wanting-as-mourning all in one.

Sitting on her bed he studied Sarah, close enough now to freeze-frame her with his eyes. Only now all he wanted to zoom in on was her face, which meant, mostly, her eyes, the rest of her body suddenly irrelevant. But, dammit, her eyes were closed, looking at the absolute secret of the world: what each of us sees when eyes are closed. Was this what he'd come for, to be frustrated again in his gaze? He closed his eyes, too, saw nothing but blank, black, dancing irritation and opened them again in a flurry of lights and motes. He let his eyes work on Sarah's mouth and her throat, her head swaying a little, moving down to her fingers, strong, firm on the keys.

The two musics, one living room one bedroom, make a gorgeous chaos—a flute-world to which Schellinger yields.

Fragments of the story of Orpheus and his lost wife swim towards him. Hell, Hades, whatever, a desolate husband, furies barring the way, a backward look—a lot of bad news. Schellinger had loved Nora, though love itself was something of a mystery and he had not paid much attention to it until she wasn't there anymore, vanished, leaving him an easy prey to self-pity and then the disaster at work.

He knew he was not one for large emotions, larger-than-life gestures, though he'd always felt larger than what he did during the day and the people he worked with—without any justification he could trust. It was probably why he was here, only he was Eurydice, lost in his own Hades, Foxx-hunting from a fuck-flick—that's what she'd called it—to this ransom by flute, if ransom was what was in the air.

Schellinger felt drained of energy; or was he simply peaceful for the first time in months? He sniffed and tasted the copper of what might be residual blood: he'd gone Foxx hunting but he was the one wounded, and he laughed a little. It was at a moment when Sarah seemed to pause for breath and opened her eyes wide.

"Don't stop," he said. "It's so beautiful."

"It's finished," she said. Her half-smile was back.

She laid the flute on the bed and they looked at each other; they were unfinished, never mind the music.

"I know the story," he said, to say something.

They held their steady look; he was thinking, how young she still looks, a kid practicing her flute; he saw the two of them, himself and Sarah, as childless children; he wondered, was Orpheus a father, Eurydice a mother?

"Everybody knows the story," Sarah said. "But that piece breaks your heart, right?"

Schellinger grabbed for his handkerchief to blot the sudden flow of blood from his nose. "Absolutely beautiful," he said. "I wish I could say beauty always makes my nose bleed, but it was you." He pasted a smile below his handkerchief. "You've always gotten to me."

She laughed a little, a first, him making her laugh.

Perched on the edge of her bed, his head tilted back against gravity's pull for his blood, he told her about his frustration at not being able to freeze-frame her. "All I had of you was this video and I wanted to get better acquainted," he said. "But if I took in one activity, I couldn't see your face; it was your smile I wanted, especially."

She was leaning back on her pillow now. "Oh," she said. "My smile."

"But if I got the smile, I couldn't see the action I wanted."

"I assume action is what that's all about."

It was important to Schellinger for Sarah to get it straight. "Not entirely," he said with the earnestness that had helped him make salesman of the year two years running. Selling was wooing, he'd always know that. "I wanted both: the erotic stuff and your smile and your eyes."

"Greedy bastard," she said. Her eyes were half-open.

"But it never worked, not the way I wanted."

She responded by telling him how she'd studied Freud, en route to becoming a music therapist—an extra use for her flute-love—and how Freud had said the voyeur is always frustrated, you can never see it fully enough, in just the right way; there has to be a feeling of complaint about what is being seen, how it's being seen; how much and for how long is always just wrong.

"Listening is more perfect," Schellinger ventured. "No frustration there. Maybe that's why it works in treating people."

Sarah was silent, eyes completely closed now, listening, but to what—the music from the living room was long since gone. When she spoke she was harsh, angry. "What is all this shit about a trip to find me because I could handle myself in some way you imagined, in that crazy scene, screwing four men and making it with that girl, Serena—how's that for a name?—I mean, you track me down so I can—what—?"

"I don't know," Schellinger said helplessly. "I didn't even know what I do know until I got here." And he sang her the old song of the life unlived, the life lived with little pleasure, finally the life that dumped you and left you.

"God," she said, "you're like that character in some play who wears black all the time because she's in mourning for her life. But that's a comic line—and you're not laughing and neither am I."

She jumped up from the bed, ran into the living room, the teddy in her hand. Schellinger watched in amazement as she began to pull her simple white blouse over her head, all the while telling him how little sympathy she has with this mourning act. "You know," she said, muffled through the fabric, "it doesn't matter what the fuck you do, it matters what you long for. What you long for is portable."

Her bra came off, lovely cup-shaped breasts, a bit fuller than he remembered, but a welcome sight.

Nevertheless, Schellinger was dazed at this new stripping surprise.

"What you long for is portable! You take it from this place, to that job . . ." She was working on the skirt now. "From this marriage to that screwed-up sex or love thing. The whole world all screwed up, trying to figure out the difference between what they do and how they feel. God! The trick is to long for something."

Impossible to ask her what was actually going on, but he found the breath to put behind a question, "And what do you long for?"

She flung her panties on top of the flute, kicked her shoes into a corner, and began to wrestle with the teddy, using a mirror near the door to help.

"Long term it's none of your business. Maybe I just want to be able to play the flute, as good as this French guy I have on the CD, Marcel Moise, do my musical therapy. I got my degree, for Christ's sake. Short term, I want you come into this bed with me, I want you to make love to me. Don't fuck me, I mean make love to me."

The teddy was tight, but Sarah was determined, muttering son-of-a-bitch, fuck, scowling into the full-length mirror. Then, success:

she turned, wheeling on her heel and toe, as in a kid's dance class. The effort had raised beads of sweat along her forehead.

"Did it! The damned thing still fits." She bowed and Schellinger rose to the occasion: he applauded, though he could see by certain bulges, tightnesses, that the teddy and Sarah lived in different times of life. Then, as she approached the bed again, he murmured, "Make love but don't fuck . . ."

"The machinery's the same," she said. "The feel is different. I mean, they're both okay in their moment. Sometimes they even shift back and forth in the same moment. But it's nice to be able to turn one off and one on. Come here."

And she turned on a smile that could light up a deserted castle.

She was chatty, afterwards, her head lying on his chest, Schellinger listening, eased, happy.

"It's not a question of regret," she spun out, a long sentence impatient of pauses, "God, I hate regret even the word re-gret I'd rather just gret if I knew what it was . . ." She snapped the teddy's shoulder strap. "Maybe I kept this little number all these years to remind me not to regret. Oh, sometimes I'm disgusted with myself for that time for doing those things with strangers and do I mean strange"—a quick shift to an old, buried rage—"they were garbage, him and his buddies who ran the show, degrading sons-of-bitches to the other girls totally. I never forgot what garbage they were even when I was putting it all behind me shoving it in a drawer I would never open again until you showed up. But I think in a funny way how you come out of things is because of who you were when you went in. I had a center, I read a lot and I thought basically people were okay maybe because I had parents who loved me and wanted equal rights for women and peace in Southeast Asia . . ." She took a breath and looked up, rolling her eyes towards Schellinger.

"Do you feel better now?" she asked. "Is this what you came hunting me for? Were you longing for this?"

Schellinger thought a moment. "No," he said. "I think what I wanted was just to find you. I thought you were—"

Sarah mocked him. "The girl of your dreams?"

A shake of the head and Schellinger said, simply, "I thought you were everything I wasn't."

"Jeez, you are solemn," she said. "And all from watching me rolling around doing various forms of the nasty." Even upside down from his chest her smile said confidence, said here I am, take it or leave it. He told her this and she jumped up to the mirror trying on different smiles. Then floating her eyes up and down, "Jesus, this thing is kind of ragged and it doesn't really fit. Nothing fits after a while—unless you're some kind of freak."

She turned back to the bed. "There's blood on the bed. You've restored my virginity. My guy's going to give that a good long laugh."

"Sorry about the bleeding," he said. "Your guy—?"

"He'll be here in an hour and a half to pick me up. It didn't occur to you I might have a guy. You figured I was waiting here all these years for you, huh? Wait a minute, gotta pee."

When she came back Schellinger was dressing, trousers, shoes and socks on, his undershirt over his head. She was not smiling now and she held the videotape in her hands.

"Here," she said. "If you want this it's okay. It seems to be the last one on earth."

Schellinger shook his head. "No," he said. "No thanks."

She tossed it onto the bed. "Listen," she said. "I'm sorry about your wife and your job. I didn't mean to be too flip about things like that." She sat down on the bed, quieter now, the run-on speeding gone. "You don't have to run so fast, there's time for you to take a shower. And you're still a little bloody." She touched his cheek. "It was kind of nice that you discovered this crazy girl and then she turned out to be me, of all people."

He reached for his shoes, perhaps prepared once again to play life's disappointed man, now the rejected, replaced lover. But Sarah would not play along. "Which means, I guess, I should say I'm sorry I tackled you like that. But I did something worse."

Distracted, he looked up. "What was that?"

"What I said about your favorite piece of music, that Debussy."

"You called it ear-soup," Schellinger said, bitterly. "But that's just talk. You don't have to apologize. What I'd really like is for you to play that Orpheus piece again."

Without hesitation she reached for her flute glimmering silver in the half-dark. Below her on the bed, Schellinger looked up at her, seeing the undercurve of her breasts, the nipples above, peeking through the teddy, and below the wink of her navel and far above the ease of that half-smile and above that the amused semicircle of her wide brown eyes. Before she would close her eyes in concentration he tried to hold it all in one glance, a polaroid freeze-frame he could take with him on the plane back. He laughed a little, remembering how Freud and Sarah had taught him it never worked, how looking was never complete enough to satisfy or to last.

Intent on playing, again, she did not notice his laugh. Schellinger lay back, half-dressed next to Sarah. Still wearing the teddy of her first mistake, now torn or decayed a little by time, she put her flute to her lips and played, her mouth elegantly pursed against the flute's opening—Orpheus pleading for his lost love to be returned to him. Schellinger listened, somnolent with satisfaction, listening with a strange sweet pleasure, to the new and nameless hidden music of longing.

Comfort

For Melissa Branfman

I was surprised she stayed in there so long with the child. She still had to soak her contact lenses before hitting the sack herself, she had to take her ulcer medicine, mixing it with grapefruit juice so that it would go down right, and I figured maybe this time I could convince her, this one night, to take a sleeping aid, something, anything even from a damn drugstore, her own sleep being even more fragile than the kid's.

We had come to the hardest place we'd known. Mary Elizabeth, who loved the sea, was now a thousand miles from water, Stonington, Kansas—the right name, stony, hard, a place without comfort. It was where her son Jamie had come out of prison a few months earlier, probably innocent of anything but an affection for turning his head around with whatever stuff he could find and bad judgment in friends.

Jamie had left us his little girl, Elizabeth, to stay until he could get back on his feet back East: printing, graphics, the stuff he'd done with a swift talent but mean results before he got in bad. Elizabeth was a tense nine-year-old, all ragged nerves from being shunted from relatives to friends, even friends of friends, and then back, and her mother dying that way. During the day she pulled it all together, flashed out a ready smile, told jokes, did puzzles I couldn't do, and read poems and such aloud to Mary Elizabeth and me.

But came time for bed, she was wired; nothing could get her off to sleep, not a night light, a hall light, quiet music. Hell, we even tried keeping the TV on without the sound, ghostly blue moving shadows in the half dark. The only answer was for her grandmother to lie with her on the bed, holding her, until the child drifted off and Mary Elizabeth could come back to her own bed.

All this would be okay except that Mary Elizabeth herself called it lucky if she got four or five hours of sleep a night; and those few hours had to be carefully worked for, with tricks and luck. TV did it sometimes for her, but she needed the sound. The talking heads could put her into a drowse which, some nights, could turn into sleep. But she sure as hell would never take a sleeping pill, nothing, not even Sominex, which you could buy at the drugstore. Some old horror of her son Jamie's addiction, a thing she never understood. In the meantime she was getting as ragged as the kid, only she was maybe fifty-three not eleven and needed the sleep more.

Movies could put her out, sometimes, if you planned for the late showing. I used to have to tell her how the movies ended over breakfast coffee the next morning. I've carried her more than once, hell, more than a dozen times, out of a movie theater, into the Dodge and then upstairs into bed. She only weighed a hundred pounds or so, having knocked off thirty pounds, easy, when the drinking stopped.

That's how we met, at the Pink Elephant, the bar where I tended and talked. I never liked to see women drink themselves sick, so I tried to distract her by telling her about my growing up near the ocean down in Pensacola and then the Merchant Marine for two years. And she told me how her folks had a potato farm in Water Mill on Long Island, and how the ocean was in her eyes and her blood for good, even though she was stuck in Stonington while her son went on trial.

"Sometimes I wake up and hear some swooshing sounds from outside," she told me, "probably just wind in the leaves, and for one lovely moment I think I'm back in my bed in Water Mill listening to the sea swoosh in the rain. There is no trouble for which the look or the sound of the sea isn't a comfort."

"Hard to get that around here," I said. "Haven't you had enough, now?"

For a bartender I'm a famously poor listener. I'm a talker all right. Even worse, I interrupt when somebody is spilling their story. Mary Elizabeth didn't seem to mind. She never told me straight out about how her son got to the point of making her life a misery, tormenting her to give him money for habits; about how he'd tried to do himself in once and how that scared her more than the other terrors. I got all this later, in bits and pieces, when we finally moved in together; or, rather, when I finally moved in with her.

I'd never seen so many books in somebody's home. Once when I was feeling a little pissy and wanting a drink myself, I asked her where reading all those books had gotten her except into the Pink Elephant and she threw one at me. I still remember it, a smallish one with a nice cover. It was called *The Go-Between*. It was not by an American.

I don't know why I came on being so proud of not being educated. I actually wanted to go back to school and Mary Elizabeth thought it was a fine idea but I've never stuck at anything very long, so neither of us was sure that I was serious about it. But I don't see where graduating in psychology from Columbia University did a whole lot to save her from a crazy life, giving up her job at Presbyterian Hospital to follow Jamie around after Elizabeth was born, because she was afraid something terrible might happen to the girl in that life, not knowing who needed her love more, the son or the granddaughter, but less and less herself and finally the drinking. She wasn't the real thing, though, getting herself off of it when Jamie went to jail, just like that; not like those of us who needed the program. Her only real dependency was her kids, both generations.

That very night, seeing how ragged she looked, I told her it was time to get a night's sleep, or she wouldn't be any good to Elizabeth the next day.

"I can't stand the idea of swallowing something to make you feel different, sleepy or anything," she said.

"I read an article," I told her, "where they said that there's never been a society can live without some kind of emotional softener, something that brings a better feeling. Even in the South Seas where it's a kind of paradise they chew betel nuts to get a regular high."

"No thanks," she said and went in to make sure the kid had brushed her teeth. In a funny way I was glad she wasn't having any of that—she was the strongest person I'd known since, maybe, my father's mother, a small, powerful woman who'd looked a little like Mary Elizabeth. I liked her independence, I liked her unyielding way of taking care while enduring shit that could have sunk a battleship.

It was hard to tell with Mary Elizabeth, but it had been a bad day, Jamie on the phone giving his time of arrival when she'd had no idea he was coming at all. He was not supposed to travel out of state without the permission of his parole officer, and who knew if he'd got that or not.

When I drove him back from the airport Jamie seemed pretty good. "New York's a bitch for graphics—designers and art directors on every street corner, but I've got me a line on a job at a trade magazine. Boats. I love doing layouts that have boats in them. You know I grew up with the ocean and the bay in my backyard. Potatoes and boats, that's my childhood." He was talking to me now, sitting next to me in the front seat, Elizabeth and the little girl in the back seat. "Do you like boats?" he asked me but never gave me a chance to say, just barreled on with, "I was supposed to get me a boat for my sixteenth birthday but I took off like a big-assed bird, instead, don't you get any ideas, kiddo," now bringing his daughter into his rapid-fire monologue. "And I never knew if I was really going to get it or not, and I was too proud to ask when the police finally brought me home.

Anyway, I'd really love this job. 'Course I think what I'd really like is to design boats, that's what I should've done, marine architects they call them. The art director said I have good hands, remember Mother, you always said I had good hands, for drawing, for fixing things, remember, Mother, I had a touch you said." But he never gave Mary Elizabeth a space to say yea or nay, just kept pile-driving words after words. "He told me if I hadn't heard from them by Wednesday I should get in touch and I call that a good sign."

He babbled on so relentlessly that my hands were tight on the wheel while I tried not to wonder what kind of state Jamie was in. Poor guy, I thought, he must be tormented by this kind of thing all the time; you get a little too quiet and people think, Christ he's too quiet, he's down and he's going to need to get high. And if he's lively and goes on and on with a pulse and a drive people like me are frozen scared, wondering is he just feeling on the upswing because somebody's maybe offering him a job or because he's back with his mother and daughter, or is he high on something and is there going to be a lot of trouble? For me, I didn't like the sound of it and I couldn't read Mary Elizabeth. I knew her various silences but I couldn't get a handle on this one, not even with a glance at her placid face in the rearview mirror.

Little Elizabeth actually got to interrupt with some success.

"Dad, Dad, hey, Dad," she threw out. "Could you draw a boat for me? The kind of boat from the bay from when you were a kid? When you were my age."

"Sure, Liz," he said. "I'll do you a two-master sailfish, soon as we land back at Grandma's place."

But when we got home he was too busy. He helped Mary Elizabeth and me with shopping and then starting a charcoal grill for the steaks; we had a kind of porch and we were allowed to use a grill if we didn't smoke the place up too much. Dinner went fine, Mary Elizabeth piling too much steak on Jamie's plate. She was both loving and a little frightened.

There was one bad moment when I was pouring the nonalcoholic beer. Jamie picked up the bottle, read the label and put it down a touch too hard. "Jesus," he said. "Some people can think of everything."

"How long will you be staying, James?" Mary Elizabeth asked quickly.

"That depends."

"On what?"

Instead of answering, he asked Mary Elizabeth to get a pad and some crayolas and he would draw little Elizabeth a sailfish. When she came back from her room, it was time for the apple pie and coffee and the drawing had to wait. But after dinner he smoked a cigarette on the porch, while Mary Elizabeth and I cleaned up, and he started a sketch. I came in, at one point, to bring in a clean ashtray and caught a glimpse—it was good, nice lines to her. "The Liz" was on the bow and he'd even put a moon in the background for luck.

I was beginning to think we might get through without the bad stuff when Mary Elizabeth hung up her apron and, in a quiet voice, said, "He's been in there too long." She meant the bathroom. It had been maybe five or six minutes, no water sounds from the sink, no flushing. Little Elizabeth was sitting with the sketch pad on her lap, as still as if someone had drawn her there: a picture of a little girl waiting for her father to come out of the bathroom and be her father again.

The first sounds were Jamie muttering things. Mary Elizabeth was at the bathroom door. "Something wrong, Jamie?"

"Nothing . . ."

"What?"

A sprinkle of broken glass and again the word "Nothing," but louder this time.

"Come on out, Jamie. Liz is waiting." She was Liz when he was around and Elizabeth the rest of the time.

"There's nothing in this fucking place. Nothing!"

Then the smashing began. Not being able to see, it sounded truly awful. Bottles certainly, maybe even the bathroom mirror, you couldn't know.

Elizabeth leaned her body against the door. I could see her trying not to cry.

"No," she called out. "There's nothing in there, Jamie. So you'd best come out and stop this. Please!" She shook the doorknob but he'd locked himself in.

She turned her head and looked at me and I went to the door and moved her away from it. I'd never done such a thing but you saw men do it in the movies a lot. I slammed my shoe hard against the bathroom door. The lock must have been flimsy, the whole apartment was sort of jerry-built, because the door snapped open as soon as I kicked. Jamie was standing there, broken glass everywhere, the sink behind him full of bottles; there was a smear of blood on one hand and on his face where he must have touched himself. And in the air such a sweet, sweet smell: he'd broken some of Mary Elizabeth's perfume bottles. Jamie was in tears, the only one of the four of us who was crying.

Mary Elizabeth pressed his hand to her lips and even with his blood smearing her face and a blankness of terror staring out of her eyes, I could see she was not going to cry. On the porch little Elizabeth never moved, just sat holding the drawing of her boat, staring at it, as if staring at something long enough, hard enough, could make it come real.

I lay on my bed waiting for Mary Elizabeth to come back in. I always waited for her to come in the bedroom before I settled down. I think she was happy about that part. I was edgy myself, that night. I wanted to ask Mary Elizabeth if maybe we could get married. I felt a little foolish, a man of forty-eight, never married. I had a kid, Jimmy, a young man of twenty-three with his own garage in Pensacola, Florida; he tried the navy for a while, then settled down to fixing cars, but I never stayed in touch with his mother, and Jimmy and I had a terrible fight, about money, I think, but I can't really remember and we're not in touch anymore, so it might as well have all never happened. Mary Elizabeth was different. She was really there, where we were. She was as much my kid as Jimmy was, even though she was older and even though we were what I suppose you could call lovers.

Also, I figured if we were married I might have more reason to go back to school, to stay in the program. But the real secret of that night for me was: I had the idea that if we were married, somehow I could do both those things, could do my life better. Maybe it was some hangover from when I was young, the idea that just being married made it possible to get a handle on the world, be taken more seriously: get a better job than making drinks at all hours, study music again, I used to have a fair tenor voice as a youngster—even move back someplace near the sea, Maine or Long Island. Or maybe I was just too scared to go it alone anymore. Being with Mary Elizabeth is what made the idea so real, anyway. Before her, it was always just an idea, something out of TV. But she was so much *there*, every day, that it made it easier to imagine going on and on.

She was going to tell me I was crazy, that she was too hung up in her troubles, a bad bet for the long haul. I knew her song by now. But I had a kind of new determination; it was blind and deaf, that determination. I was counting on that, so I could convince her to see it with my eyes, not her own.

I stepped into the hallway and looked into the child's bedroom; the door was half open and I could see the two of them lying slantwise across the bed in a tangle of blankets and stuffed animals, the girl stirring and whispering something, Mary Elizabeth absolutely still. I stepped in further to see if maybe it was time for her to come back in. She caught me at the edge of her vision and waved me away.

It went that way two more times. And now we were at maybe a half hour after midnight. Mary Elizabeth was still wearing the pants and sweater she'd worn all day. I tried to get her out, several times again, figuring the kid was asleep by now, it's time to get her out. In the past she's always tiptoed out leaving Elizabeth sprawled, mouth open, breathing and dreaming God knows what. But this time she only kept waving me off.

The last time was at almost three A.M. I'd dozed off with the lights still blazing away and woke up, confused. Then I remembered where I was and I went to the doorway and looked in.

"Hey," I whispered. "Mary Elizabeth. Hey, come on. She's okay now."

The child was safely wrapped in a tangled nest of sheets and blankets. She was even snoring a little. When Mary Elizabeth heard me she raised her head and gave me the fiercest look I'd ever seen. Then one last wave for me to go away and she went back to holding onto her granddaughter, curved against her, holding on with a grip as fierce as that look she'd just given me. I don't know how anybody could sleep held in a grip like that!

And standing in the hallway, alone, I saw my mistake. She was not holding on, hour after hour, to comfort the child, giving up the few hours of sleep she would need so much the next day when she'd surely be exhausted and empty-eyed. No! It was Mary Elizabeth who needed the comfort of the little girl, holding tightly to the small curve under the blankets even though she was now deeply asleep and apparently couldn't know she was being held with such faithfulness. It was the grown woman lost in her life who held onto the child and wanted to lie there all night, waving me away, needing the touch of the small body and its breathing, regular at last, comfort flowing the other way now, impossible to separate the two in the confusion of blankets and bears.

How wrong you can be about people, even people you thought

you loved or wanted to marry. I turned off the lights and lay in the dark, breathing too hard, frightened at how little I knew. And I wondered if it wasn't too late to change, to let some softness into my hard life; to call my own son, Jimmy, and tell him I was sorry I didn't lend him the money to buy his first house, thinking it was too much money, too damned fancy a house for the kid, but that was none of my business, either give somebody or don't give, but don't preach—wondering if it wasn't too late to listen to Mary Elizabeth instead of talk; and I remembered all the times I'd given up on people or let them give up on me because I became like stone, deaf and cold, impossible to give or get comfort, and I rolled over on my side on the bed, clutching the pillow to my chest, letting out small weird sounds of misery, of regret.

Mary Elizabeth stood in the doorway looking at me, bleary-eyed, amazed at the sight of me in some kind of fit.

"What is it?" she said. "What's wrong?"

And how was I to tell her that I was scared it might be too late—most of all too late to become the kind of man who might find out who this woman was who was letting me join her life; to learn who it was who needed comfort so much she had to take it from a sleeping child, lying on that bed like an island in the ocean she loved, now so far away, so long ago?

Imperato Placeless

The chest pains began when he was in the middle of the interview with the kid from Artforum. The interviewer was not really a kid but at seventy-eight Imperato had gotten into the habit of calling anybody a kid who hadn't been a grownup in the forties and fifties.

At first it had felt like heartburn, general internal irritation, so he could blame it on the young man with the fancy Mont Blanc pen. ("I don't believe in taping," he'd announced on arriving at the hotel room. "An interview should be an encounter.") An encounter was not exactly what Imperato had in mind for his first trip back to New York from his weird new life in Wisconsin. Clearly Miles was going to be a pain-in-the-ass, but Imperato had to admit he was an informed pain-in-the-ass. He'd done his homework, knew which biography of Pollock was bullshit and by what percentage; knew the Rothko estate battle by heart; had spoken to Ruth Kligman and Larry Rivers—had had an exchange of letters with Phil Gustin's widow, Musa.

He was maybe twenty-eight so the New York School, the abstract expressionists, whatever, was something he'd read about, learned at school. And here Imperato loomed before him lighting cigarettes from old butts, a six-foot-three grayed-out lion in the path:

71

art history on the hoof. "The main survivor of New York," the kid had called him. "I see New York in everything you do. Every color choice, every passage of the brush. Even though you've broken it down the way Mondrian broke down music—New York is to you what Giverney was to Monet. You are the great painter of the city."

"Hey," Imperato said. "Great is a bullshit word. It's staying power, doing the work. And don't forget. Monet invented Giverney. I didn't start New York. It was here when I was born."

"I'm not so sure," the kid said. His name was Paul Miles, a poet, he told Imperato right off, maybe trying to get empathy, smooth cooperation. He was only moonlighting in journalism, he said, uncertain about getting his doctorate—teaching and poetry fighting for their share. He confided the central problem of his life in two minutes, New York style, that the only places he could do graduate studies and get his Ph.D. were Illinois, Iowa, Montana. And he was fearful that his poetry would die on him if he were not connected to his place, to New York. "The Battery Park series—abstract or not—those paintings reinvent New York. The skyline as hallucination, broken down to geometric fragments, but they still stop your heart the way the skyline does if you've been away from the city for a long time and you come in from Kennedy and go past Queens over the Triborough Bridge."

"Where are the matches, you seen the matches?"

"If you have chest pains you shouldn't be smoking . . ."

"I didn't even come from New York. Forget the Triborough, I came across the Brooklyn Bridge. Longest trip in the world . Where are the matches. You see those matches anywhere?"

It was Imperato's first trip back to New York after relocating, starting again, ending up, call it what you like, in Madison, Wisconsin. His life had been ripe for dramatic change after his divorce from Sylvana. Everybody had something to tell him about the importance of change. Susan Levy, his new dealer, had told him that for him the need to go on living in New York was moot. It was one of her favorite words, ex-lawyer that she was.

"You don't need it the way you used to. It's in your blood by now. Wherever you are is New York. It's a permanent fact in you. Teaching in the Midwest will give you a new push." Not so different from what the interviewer said. Everybody seemed to be singing that song these days.

He'd been dumb, had made dumb investments, a dumb third marriage to an eager Sylvana who'd been eager to learn, eager to marry, to divorce, eager to rack up a giant divorce settlement: cash, paintings—what a mess. When the offer from Wisconsin arrived it seemed like a great idea. India Claire seemed to have arrived at the same time, restless, eager only to help him; a throwback to the fifties, all those painters' women and wives submerged in their men and their work, carving out their own ambitions in secret, nights and Sundays; eternally shadowed. The opposite of Sylvana. It was not clear if it was getting involved with India which had led to teaching at the University or if she was just another symptom of a need for a new way of being in the world. Anyway she was a postdoctoral fellow at the University and she knew where to find a house with a separate studio, knew where to find the particular kind of parmesan cheese Imperato liked, knew when to keep quiet about his painting.

Almost immediately after setting up his studio and teaching his first students, he'd had to return to New York for the interview. The new show at Susan Levy's gallery was coming up and Artforum wanted to do a memory piece, photograph him at the old places: the Cedar Bar, the building where the Club used to meet on Friday nights, Betty Parsons, the old Stable Gallery. They were mostly ideas now, memories, not places any more. The Cedar had moved, several blocks up from the old address on University Place; Betty Parsons was gone, the Stable long closed. It was all enough to give anybody heart pains or heartburn, whatever it was.

To make things worse, the snow had followed him from Wisconsin, threatening to become a blizzard, to blanket his return pilgrimage in silent, shivery white. The dampness made the arthritis in his right hand worse. God, the great comedian, had sent the almost crippling effect to the painting hand. Imperato had put the operation off as long as possible. "Good news," he'd told India, zipping out of the surgeon's examination room. "They can't operate until they're sure my heart can take it." It was hard to tell good news from bad these days. In his secret darkest concerns he was terrified that he'd not be able to paint anymore. A concern he sure as hell was not going to share with any snotnosed kid interviewer.

"Listen," he said to Miles, "how about we look at some pictures. We can do the interview on the hoof."

"Are you feeling okay enough? We don't have a lot of time before we have to meet this photographer."

"Enough," Imperato said. He'd found the matches and the consolations of smoke eased him. "My bags are at Susan Levy's. We can just go."

"How long has she been your dealer?"

"You ever wonder that the word for drug pushers and art gallery people is the same word? Cheap shot, skip that. Two years, since Klemtner. Same dealer for thirty years. Only bad thing he ever did to me was die."

Imperato was eager to get out of the hotel, uneasy, he didn't quite know why.

"Why did you leave your bags at the gallery instead of here?"

"This isn't a here," Imperato said, gruff, concluding his cigarette. "This is a hotel in New York."

They went to the Mondrian show at MOMA. Miles had this hushed reverence maybe because Imperato had hung out with Mondrian, for a while—those hopped-up years of the war—Pete, they'd all called him, juiced on jazz, incongruous in those somber gray suits of his, the two Dutchmen, de Kooning and Mondrian, circling each other warily at the Cedar Bar.

Imperato had his own way of looking at pictures, whipping from one to the other, then settling down for an endless look at one particular item. Miles glanced at his watch. "We have exactly fifty minutes until we have to meet the Artforum photographer at the Cedar's."

"Look at this," Imperato said, holding in front of one of the Boogie-Woogie series. "You look at this organized space and you can forget about time." Then on to another room, going backwards, now the young Mondrian painting trees. then on to the stripped-down geometric paintings. "You see how you get the feeling that it cost him something to eliminate, to get down to bedrock. Every step he took he paid a price."

Miles scribbled notes. "Did you pay a price for moving away from the figure and then back again?"

"Ah, what the hell do I know about why I do something. You know why I paint certain pictures? Because I look at a Tiepolo, or Milton Avery—and suddenly I want to do one of my own."

"You mean painting comes from painting?"

"Sort of. The way an itch comes from scratching."

The room was suddenly full of Japanese tourists carefully taking photographs, framing the paintings, careful not to use the forbidden flash. "Reminds me," he says. "Kuniyoshi was so big in the forties and fifties. Nobody looks at those pictures anymore, those elegant golfers. Don't always know who's going to come up or stay down." He was annoyed at the crowding, the idea of tourism in a place for paintings, though none of them spoke above a whisper or intruded into his looking space. At the corner there was a window swabbed with flying snow. In the next room were some of Mondrian's earliest work, they were going backwards, Imperato's personal way of wandering through a show, and he was stoned silent by the shaping hand in those early trees whose destiny was, finally, to be whittled down to taped lines enveloping space and light.

He was relieved when Miles said, suddenly, "Listen, I have to go to the bathroom. I have some kind of bladder infection, antibiotics and all that stuff. Be right back."

Miles was replaced by a surge of the Japanese and German tourists. This time they flowed between Imperato and the pictures he wanted to see. But his brisk irritation was quickly replaced by a slower, deeper anger. They were floaters in New York, in and out of museums, restaurants, constantly counting out tips in alien currency, laughing at the wrong times at jokes in a strange language, going back to rest in hotel rooms in the suspended transient air of late afternoon, weightless, floating, drifting.

And he, Imperato—what the hell was he doing going back to a hotel in New York? He'd worn out whole chunks of New York real estate, the loft on Wooster Street, the apartment on Eighth Street before Eighth Street went honky-tonk, the co-op on 81st near Park when Klemtner started to sell paintings at an outrageous price—for a while. He'd claimed whole neighborhoods with his feet, walking from river to river, through Central Park, gobbling the city with strides, with eyes, sleepwalking the galleries, returning to his loft, his apartment, his digs, wherever, to work, body worn out, hands ready to make something out of his street-and-gallery-gaze. How the hell had he landed back in town without a place of his own for the first time in fifty years!

He fled the room, the cameras, the Japanese and Germans who were alien mainly in that they were not from New York. And there, in his refuge, gazing at de Chirico's astonishing girl rolling a hoop down a deserted street, was Susan Levy and a man in a tweed jacket, tall, proprietary. As Imperato watched, the man's hand touched Susan's arm lightly to make a point, the real point being the right to touch her in a certain way, all of it adding immensely to Imperato's irritation.

"Susan," he boomed in a spell-shattering, un-museum voice. "What the hell are you doing here?"

She kept that cool poise of hers, making introductions (Imperato deliberately not registering the tweed jacket's name). "Just checking up on the competition."

They strolled on *a trois*; when he fell behind a moment Imperato took in the sleek curve of her legs, short skirt enhancing the effect, her small breasts, so much more subtle than India's full endowment. Gazing at the elegant indentation of her waist Imperato felt a sudden surge of lust, a quickening in the groin and the pulse, hard to say which came first. At the same time he thought of the mysteries of time—how old had Susan been when he'd broken up with whatsher-name Leah who'd then tried suicide—Susan then maybe eight years old. God! When she first menstruated he'd been at least thirty-five, a lot of life behind him, a whole life ahead of him, as it turned out. Anyway, all that was moot now, the word as interpreted to him by Susan fascinated Imperato. A word that told you no matter how important or urgent something might feel, at a certain moment it could have no practical effect, could change nothing, make nothing happen; in effect, didn't matter.

On the other hand he didn't feel moot. Imperato had never felt anything to be moot in his life. And he refused to think even his star-tling tremble of lust for Susan might be. He and India had a pretty good lust going, the sexual play doing nicely. Unlike the arthritis in his painting hand, that part of his life had not served him notice. But Susan was his dealer; a tricky confusion of realms. In a panic he thought he saw Miles at the entrance to the room, turned and low-ered his head, but it was not him. The moment made Imperato realize that it was not only the Germans and the Japanese he had fled, it was Miles, the photography session, the interview. He wasn't inter-ested in his past. Let the dead bury the dead, was that how it went?

The pictures slid by in a haze, now, while Imperato was on an internal binge of doubt and change. He realized, with great clarity, how much he did not want to marry India. He cared about her, probably loved her, but marriage, no! Why? Because her breasts were too large compared to Susan Levy's small elegant ones? Lunacy. But he suddenly did not want to leave a widow. And this thought became mysteriously mixed with the paintings waiting to be hung at Susan Levy's gallery. He wanted to see them all again before anyone else could look at them.

They had all paused, looking at Matisse's flat red room. Giddy, he thought: what did painters all have, after all, except shape, color, light, and air. He remembered the composer Morty Feldman joking at the Cedar's, "Beethoven, Mozart . . . Take away the scale and the Alberti bass and what do they have?" Sweet Jesus, take away shape, color, light, air . . . But Imperato was visualizing his own paintings waiting to be photographed at the gallery and he was filled with anxiety, didn't like the evenness of the forms, was afraid he might have slipped into some kind of easy geometric look at space.

Imperato struggled with this panic. Easy does it, he thought. You've had these feelings before. He concentrated on the walls filled with shape, color, light, air. Behind him two men maneuvered into a place to better see the paintings. But Jesus God almighty, one of them had swollen, blueish eyes, three-quarters closed, and carried a white cane. The other man was short, intense, wearing a purple tie the museum should have confiscated on the way in, an offense to the idea of color. He projected a low, insistent buzz and Imperato realized he was describing the paintings to the blind man. A first! Art criticism replacing the act of looking. Description—God, how did you describe a color, this short guy with a purple tie had better be the greatest poet the English language had ever produced if he wanted to duplicate the act of seeing a painting. A wisp of a guilty feeling presented itself— for God's sake, not being able to see. What could be worse?

That did it! He took Susan Levy's hand and pulled her a few steps away from the tweed jacket. One of their hands was damp, one was dry, he couldn't tell which but he could guess.

"Hey, Susan," he whispered, hearing his voice hiss loudly in his ears, "I have to get into the gallery and see the paintings."

She looked at him oddly; she was cool, not sharing his apparent panic. He realized she did not know him very well; Klemtner had known how to ride out his ups and downs.

"I can't leave now. This is a client. And they're coming to photograph the show in a few hours."

"Great. That gives me a little time. Let me have a key and meet me there when you can."

"God, Imperato." She detached a key from a ring. "Don't do anything crazy. I'll get there as soon as I can."

On 53rd Street he did see Miles, waiting in the windblown snow, scanning faces. Imperato ducked into the lobby, through the bookstore, poster hell, kitsch heaven he thought as he hailed a cab, his back to the crowd in the vortex of which Miles the poet/journalist waited. Lust for Susan Levy was quickly replaced by guilt for Miles. He would make it up to the kid, somehow, he thought as the cab crawled through midtown traffic.

By the time he got to the gallery he was ripe for all sorts of change and trouble.

The gallery was rich with the smell of fresh paint—many of the paintings were only weeks old. What he wanted, actually, was the smell of his studio; the difference was mainly the absence of the coppery smell of turps. Imperato threw his snow-soaked coat on a chair in Susan's little office off the main section of the gallery. There was a small fridge in a corner of the office and from this he extracted a bottle of cold Pinot Grigio Susan kept to celebrate and seal a sale. He sat and sipped wine from a plastic cup not ready to start turning paintings around, wondering why he was here, why feeling the same as a bunch of German and Japanese tourists in New York, in the same hotel-bound floating situation, and then being freaked by a blind man looking at paintings should make him question everything, the show about to be hung, getting married to India when he'd suddenly rather make love to Susan Levy. It was bad enough to leave walking around New York to move to Wisconsin and start driving everywhere, but seeing New York only from the outside made him feel outside everything; it was all too much.

One by one he turned the paintings around. It was as he'd feared. The shapes were wrong. In the middle of his journey around the gallery Susan Levy marched in. Alone. At least one good thing had happened—she'd dumped the tweed jacket. But she was pissed.

"What the hell is going on, Imperato?"

He did not know the answer to that question so he ducked it. "Did I ever tell you how I got drunk as a skunk at Franz Kline's place around 1952, when he first began to do the big black-and-white larger-than-life calligraphy? I wasn't ready for that. I didn't want to give up on color and the shapes were so far from the body it gave me an anxiety attack. Everything is calligraphy except when you start from the body."

Susan rubbed her hands together to get rid of the chill.

"You got a sketch pad and a cigarette?"

"A sketch pad, yes. You are a great painter, but even a great painter can't smoke here, you know that."

That word great again. It made everybody in the art world comfortable, everybody except the artists, except Imperato. "Okay, I'll take the pad."

While sketching some ellipsoids he asked Susan to call the Cedar Bar and tell the kid he'll be over soon; apologize, make some excuse, not feeling well.

She looked at him shrewdly, neatly plucked eyebrows raised. "Are you sick, is something wrong?"

He said nothing, crumpled a page to the floor and started again.

He was not sure exactly what he was doing. But he did not tell

Susan that he wanted to take pieces out of the show, maybe delay the whole business until he got it right. He didn't like the smoothness, the evenness of the forms.

He swiftly covered a page with ellipsoids, not caring if they overlapped, scribbled onto each other. That was the natural shape of the human body as a still life . . . With no arm or leg extended—at rest . . . He took a swig of Pinot Grigio, took his life in his hands and when she hung up the phone he said, "Susan—I need you to pose for me."

"Now? Here?"

"Right," he said.

Susan stared over his shoulder examining the sketch pad. He could see she was stalling.

"I never told you but I used to pose nude at the Art Students League on 57th Street . . ."

"For Christ's sake, I know where the Art Students League is . . ." But he stared at her in surprise.

"I was sending myself through NYU Law School."

"You never mentioned it to me . . ."

"I never mentioned it to any of my artists."

"I'm not 'any' of your artists." He studied her as if she were already undressed. There was something nicely curved and solid about Susan.

"I didn't want to muddy the artist-dealer relationship."

All Imperato could think—and then say—was: "If you'd pose for those snotnose kids smelling of turps . . ."

"I tried to work up the nerve to tell my nice Jewish mother, just to shock her, to tell her she didn't know everything about me." She grinned. "You smell the same way, Imperato. Only you became a great artist and they—"

"Oh, Christ," he said, "don't start with that 'great' business. I'm still learning, so . . ."

She hovered in front of him and held up a diamond-studded

watch on a thick wrist. "Photographers are coming in a half-hour," she said, her mouth curving in wry disbelief, "and you want me to take off my clothes in my gallery at three o' clock in the afternoon and pose nude?"

Sketching the curve of her breast, using charcoal to smudge the edges a bit, Imperato felt his foolish afternoon lust dissipating into the pleasure, the passionate, complicated difficulty, of drawing her body. He hadn't even asked for an easel, stood her instead in front of the desk where he sat, the sketch pad on his lap . . . Susan standing, arms at her side, slightly turned away from his gaze.

Yes, he thinks, the ellipsoid . . . remembering Mantegna, Tintoretto . . . That first trip to Florence and Venice after the war . . . How wiped out he'd been by the way they lowered the body of Jesus, the descent from the cross in the murals in the Ca'd'Oro . . . Nobody understood that it wasn't how you broke with the past that mattered so much . . . It was how you took your move from the past . . . How you tied yourself to the old guys and then cut the rope . . . Some plunged down . . . And some found a place to stand in midair.

Something to do with the sense of placelessness. Maybe it didn't matter if your beaten-up, arthritic body was in New York or Madison. Finally, the body is the only place we have. Imperato began to laugh. He'd discovered the truth of his old age. To hell with the Germans and the Japanese and their hotels. He was not placeless, after all. It was why he'd never quite left the figure all those years when everybody had given up on it, just a few staying on, Larry, Pearlstein, the wild men in England, Bacon, Freud.

Susan shivered. "Enough, Imperato, how about it?"

To distract her he asked, "What is this word you like so much, moot. You said it was moot where I lived, where I painted, New York or Wisconsin. Such a funny sound."

"I picked it up when I was a lawyer—more of a lawyerette, I never got very far but at least I learned how to do a contract—anyway, it's when it doesn't pay to argue anymore because the crucial moment has passed or when you can't win by going on making distinctions."

"Moot," Imperato muttered.

"It's chilly in here. You know I have never taken such a crazy chance in broad daylight. But I think you're the best I've got." She folded her arms around her waist for warmth. "If you want to feel special, now you know how special. Listen, we've got a big day coming up."

But he wasn't in a mood for big days, in no mood to listen, only to look. "Turn a little to the left," he said, thinking he would get over his guilty feelings about having dumped Miles by giving him advice: tell the kid it didn't matter where he spent his life. Tell him it doesn't matter a damn if he stays in journalism, goes into teaching or not: it was all moot, Susan's wonderful lawyer's word. If he's going to write poems he'll write them any which way—Wallace Stevens at the insurance office or Hart Crane drunk on a village floor. All that's just living. He imagined Miles asking him, with that eager probe of a voice, had he known Hart Crane and he would reply hell, no, I was still a baby in the twenties.

Or maybe you had to spend your life, one way or another, and then find out it didn't matter where, that you and your place were the same thing. Moot, he thought, the word repeating itself in his head over and over, mootmootmootmootmootmoot . . . it emptied his mind and let him connect his gaze with his hand sweeping furiously, his index finger curved like a broken scimitar, his thumb jabbing pains at him, Imperato too busy, too triumphant in everything he'd learned, to register small pains.

The ringing of the phone seemed to galvanize Susan—a blare from the outside world that reminded her she was standing naked in her own gallery in the middle of the afternoon. She grabbed for the phone and for her blouse and underwear at the same time.

"It's India," she breathed at Imperato.

"I'm not here," he said. "I'm not here."

"He's not here, India," Susan lied, and of a sudden it almost became the truth. Imperato had fallen across the desk, one gnarled hand clutching charcoal, had fallen across the blurry images of Susan's body—his consciousness was slipping. The ringing of the doorbell was the newest ring and suddenly everyone else was there, Paul Miles and a short photographer in a black leather jacket lugging tons of equipment, lights and stuff, and Susan was struggling into her blouse and skirt, embarrassed as hell, ignoring the bra, stuffing it into a desk drawer just beneath Imperato's nose. Imperato took all this in even though the chest pains had gone from small to large, even though his vision was blurring.

He pushed himself up from the desk, wanting to thank Susan for posing for him, for covering for him with India. But for the moment his breath was modest, available only in small bursts. He wanted to tell Paul Miles that the paintings are not to be photographed, that they're not right yet, Imperato can do better. But, for the moment, such questions are moot and he settled for grabbing Susan by the shoulders. As if touching her was curative, the pains recede and he thought with longing about a cigarette.

Susan chanted, "Imperato, are you all right, are you all right?" Her embarrassment at being caught posing naked in the afternoon at her own gallery was replaced by anxiety. Imperato stood erect trying, by an act of will, to inhabit well the only place he has left, his towering, arthritic body. And flushed with all he had lately learned, he managed to squeeze out two words.

"I'm great," Imperato said, refusing for a moment to die and hoping she did not misunderstand.

Chaos

For Joshua Branfman

They are driving home from the wedding, Carl and Terry's formal festivities, when the fight starts. Nothing at the wedding could have triggered it. Mickey hasn't neglected Madge; he hasn't drunk too much. The afternoon has dazzled their eyes with sun and the classical forms of June white gowns and white dinner jackets; there have been stately processions and stuffy toasts. But when the first tremors begin, before they hit the freeway, Mickey knows it is going to be the same old complaint; the familiar engine which has driven so many of the collisions in their two-year adventure. It begins with a deceptive softness.

"It's chaos," Madge murmurs.

"Oh, God."

"Never mind Oh God."

"I just mean—why now? Today is no more chaotic than any other day."

"Exactly so," she says. It is one of his lawyer's turns of phrase she's picked up.

"Get your own lines. Exactly so is usually followed by Your Honor."

"Today was a symphony of order. It reminded me how crazy our life is."

"You mean today was marriage. Marriages are rituals, rituals are emblems of order. Fine. Let's get married."

Madge drums her fingers on the armrest, a mini-bolero of misery. That kind of glib reply, she tells him, is why they hold the world's record for breakups during a two-year relationship.

"Please," Mickey says. "Don't call it a relationship. Call it an affair, a *sordid* affair, an arrangement—anything but a relationship. Talk like a musician, not a social worker. Besides, there was a fair amount of chaos out there. Carl headed for you and ended up kissing me on the ear."

"That's because I ducked. I think you missed the turnoff."

He doubles back, illegally crossing the solid white line. Romances *and* breakups flower at weddings. Everyone knew that. He should have expected the trouble. The chaos and disorder of his life drove her wild, as it has so often in the past—that was at the heart of it. They've been together for two years, interrupted by five breakups. Once he'd enraged her by pointing out that the way they lived, on-again, off-again, her walking in and out of the door, was also a kind of chaos.

At home, Madge seems to shift gears by silently getting out of her pink and white wedding outfit and into slacks and a sweater. Then she comes out of the bedroom with a handful of papers in her hands. She says, "Mickey, I'm leaving. I mean, for good." She hands him the papers. "There's a five o'clock flight to L.A. Here, these are some of your notes from class. I found them in my underwear drawer."

"Maybe they belong in your underwear drawer," he says even though his stomach tells him it may be too late for jokes. "Maybe *I* belong there. Please don't leave. Why today, why now?"

Over her slow, implacable packing Mickey weaves a web of plea bargaining. How much they have in common. Okay, he isn't a patch on her as a pianist, but if Bogart and Bergman would always have

Paris, they would always have the Beethoven Archduke Trio, over which they'd met, Madge playing with two friends of Mickey's. Where would she find another lawyer with whom she could play the heartbreaking Schubert duo for four hands in F minor? But she could, it seemed, do without lawyers forever. The third suitcase slams shut. Besides, she points out, he hasn't achieved that exalted status yet, and may never.

She turns and nails him: "This crazy chaos is going to destroy any chance you have to *become* a lawyer. What do they think about you at Columbia—a second-year law student who never shows up on time and is two papers behind in every class?"

It does not seem the perfect moment to tell her that he is far from sure, anymore, that he wants to be a lawyer. He'd fallen into law school the way he fell into most things—a kind of clever inertia. He had the grades in college and his smarter friends were doing it; much of the nation had been going to law school. Now the newspapers are full of articles about the law glut—lawyers not practicing law, frantically looking for jobs. It gives him the sense of being adrift in a boat with the course not quite set. It also makes him wonder if today's order—law school followed by a clerkship followed by a job search—might not simply be tomorrow's confusion.

Mickey tries to help her lug the suitcases into the foyer but she fights him off. In desperation he tells her, "Drop the suitcases!" The unexpectedness of the command works. She drops them and stands staring wildly while he speaks.

"Do you have any idea how much pain all of this disorder gives *me?*"

"Gives *you*—"

"Me! The hours spent looking for pieces of paper that mean life or death, passing or failing."

"Hours? Years!" she says.

"Years—okay, years! And the years seesawing from one project to another before I land somewhere. Did I tell you I was the oldest in my class? Thirty-six and still nowhere."

He does not really feel as badly about this as he is implying. But he is terrified that this one might be the breakup that lasts, that loses her for good. It has the signs. She's never packed so quickly any of the other times.

"You don't have a tenth of your stuff there. Madge, where are you going?"

"I told you, L.A. I'll stay with my sister. I'll get studio work, recording. It's where I got my big assignment. I should probably live there, anyway." L.A. was where she'd fled each time. She was wired into the West Coast music network. During her last flight a friend had gotten her a special gift: to write music for a documentary on the fall of communism. It got an Academy Award nomination—her first time out.

"You're forgetting how much you hate being in the sun all the time."

"Maybe I'll get lucky. I'll be inside working."

"You'll work day and night," he says, contradicting himself, desperate. "You are the classiest music act they can find out there among the oranges." He takes a beat and inadvertently stops trying to con her. "Talent like yours doesn't grow on trees," he tells her, so eager to please that he is mangling oranges and musical talent in one hodgepodge.

She shrugs. "I haven't done much with it. That reminds me: I left most of my sheet music."

"You can't go without that."

"Stuff you can ship. People just have to leave!"

Mickey takes a chance. He argues with all the persuasiveness he can bring to the job, that if she is going to go, then they should split up their possessions now. There isn't that much, mostly books and records. There is the piano but you couldn't chop it up and give forty-four keys to each of them, so that could wait. He is playing for time. She probably knows it but it doesn't seem to matter.

He makes them coffee and they sit in the middle of the living room surrounded by assorted objects: clocks and other tabletop items, laptop computers owned in common, but mostly mounds of books and records. It starts off neatly with the books, Mickey giving up Donald Tovey on Beethoven, Madge giving up the biography of Janis Joplin: a feast of politesse.

By they time they get to the real music, she actually smiles now and then. "God, you forget how much you collect. I didn't know we had this early Billie Holliday."

The music collection was mostly cassettes. They are living on a short string and it was cheaper to record from the radio onto cassettes than to buy CDs. It had been Mickey's idea to build a pirated library, taken from the airwaves. By now he has forgotten who first taught him the trick of pasting a little piece of Scotch tape over the holes at the top of an audio cassette, so that you could record over whatever was on it, ad infinitum. Whoever it was, he'd always thought, deserved the Nobel Prize for victimless white collar crime.

An hour later his strategy shows signs of working. Madge lies on the floor on her side, propped up by an elbow. Mickey has dragged out a portable player to try out various cassettes. The Schumann Piano Concerto pacifies the air. Madge sighs along with the music. Then follows the Mozart A Minor Sonata for Two Pianos.

"Our song," Mickey says.

"We never played that."

"We could have. We still could. You're breaking up a great duo-piano team."

"We had a plan to save up enough money to get another piano and a bigger apartment. But you never stuck to the savings plan. A savings plan needs order, regularity. And a duo-piano team needs two pianos."

She changes cassettes. In the middle of the Beethoven Seventh, the slow movement wiping her out and giving Mickey a quick false hope, an announcer's voice cuts in, like a voice from another planet, then come quick cuts of other pieces of music blurring by, then silence. Colder and colder, she tosses cassettes on, jabs buttons and hears more and more confusion of music, voices and gibberish.

By the fourth one she goes crazy.

"Shit!" Madge says. "Look at these. You've recorded over every beautiful thing in the world." She stands up, cassettes raining all around her. She is crying now. This is bad! Only two martinis, only a child being hurt on television news can make Madge cry. She grabs him by the hand threatening the connection between Mickey's arm and its socket and runs him on a wild tour through the four rooms of the apartment.

"Look at that pile of books on the floor. LOOK! It's been there since last summer. Do you think you *know* which books are there?" Mickey says nothing, lets himself be dragged from room to room, hoping it will end soon. She throws open the doors to his closet, shining the spotlight of her outraged eyes on the mess of mismatched shoes, gleaming amid the occasional pair of pants on the floor of the closet, a dusty debris of old suspenders, forgotten ties, a crushed aluminum music stand next to a legal dictionary he'd been looking for, for weeks. To the left of the closet a fax machine has bled white papers onto the floor without the blessing of a paper tray.

She looms above it all, an outraged goddess of order pronouncing judgment on a world of confusion. *"Chien-lit!"* she cries into a world she never made. *"Chien-lit!"*

Mickey finds his voice at this. "What's that? You don't speak French!" As if, on the eve of losing her, he cannot bear the idea that he may not have really known her—a lover with a secret addiction to speaking French.

"It means dog-in-the-bed. My father used to say that. He stole it from General de Gaulle."

"Your father knew de Gaulle? A psychiatrist from Claremont, California, knew the president of France?"

"It was in the papers in '68. When the students rioted in the streets, in Paris. De Gaulle said, *'Reform, oui, Chien-lit, non!'* I was a kid and I knew the French words for dog and bed. I thought *Chien-lit* meant dog in the bed. To a kid it seemed like a terrific way to describe complete confusion. Anyway, when all of France was boiling over into chaos that's what de Gaulle called it. My father never forgot it. To me it's always going to be dog-in-the-bed."

Mickey says, bemused, "You told me he terrorized you and your sister."

"Maybe. But he was right about a lot of things."

On the way to the suitcases in the living room Mickey tells her he can reform and she tells him *he* is the dog in her bed. She stands for a moment surrounded by what seems to be thousands of audio cassettes. She stoops and picks one up. It is unlabeled: it could contain all the recorded beauty in the world—or all the silence. There is no way to know.

"Mickey," she says. "You've recorded over every piece I loved—and probably some that you loved. And you never changed any of the labels—if they have any labels at all. You couldn't find something you wanted to hear no matter how hard you tried. That's not a music collection. That's chaos recording over love."

"All this is about cassettes? Come on, Madge!"

"You'll never get the idea."

"It started with Carl and Terry getting married."

"No, that's how it ended. You'll never get it."

"Let's us get married. This is Mickey and Madge we're talking about."

She reaches the door and turns back. "Your name is supposed to be Michael. What kind of a name is Mickey for a grown man? My God!"

Mickey knows better now than to prolong the struggle. If it's reached names it's over. He lets her go.

The next morning Mickey wakes up at five A.M. A good three hours before his usual time. Ah, he thinks, Madge is in L.A. and I'm on California time, too. He eats wildly, two glasses of orange juice, two bowls of cereal, two cups of coffee: he is eating for both of them. Then, too restless to study for class, he returns to the scene of last night's crime.

He goes to a desk drawer in his bedroom and, as if by some atavistic instinct, finds a bunch of labels he'd bought so long ago that there is a serious question about the enduring stickiness of the gummed side. He will perform a kind of magic trick: he will lock the barn door now that the horses of his love are gone. He will execute a feat of order, lovely in its belatedness; an argument for the persistence of hope.

He borrows Madge's ears and plays cassette after cassette, surprised at what he hears. Once you become someone else, even for a moment, you are utterly vulnerable. Things he would never have noticed are, in a moment, awful scratches on his soul—like a wonderful old recording of the Mozart E minor violin sonata played by Szymon Goldberg and Lili Krauss, both now asleep with Mozart, which suddenly just stops. It does not end—it cuts off right in the middle of the slow movement, in the middle of an exquisite dying, descending phrase.

He had tried explaining to Madge that when you record from the radio, while you're working at your desk, studying to become a Supreme Court justice, starting first as a lawyer of course, you couldn't time the random arrival of a piece on the radio compared to how much tape was left. You just hit the record button so you wouldn't lose it, and you got as much as you got. Madge told him that the process didn't matter. It was the rotten result: the frustration of expectation as you listened—a kind of musical premature ejaculation, leaving her frustrated and edgy with unsatisfied yearning.

He has never gotten to properly explain to Madge that something in him *likes* the shock of surprise at accidentally coming on a piece of music, even a part of one, unexpectedly; that something in him rebels against the divine principle of Alphabetical Order; he has never explained it to himself either. Even though it is one of the great cushions against the pain and confusion of daily life. Once you gave up on alphabetical order you were ready for anything—or nothing. It was like giving up on the Judeo-Christian Ethic.

Could he, Mickey wondered, skip the Law and become a Piano Bum now that Madge was out of his life? He can play a modest version of every standard from Jerome Kern to the Beatles. Why not? Live a life of requests and tips, an unfinished vodka always waiting on the piano. Maybe it was only Madge in his life, Madge next to him in bed, Madge over the coffee cups, Madge on the phone or at the piano that had kept him on the straight and narrow, or as straight and as narrow as he had been.

He wanders into the kitchen, absently holding an unlabeled cassette, and pours his third cup of coffee. If he does call Madge he will be so wired by caffeine God knows what the conversation will be like.

A few moments later he is playing fragments of cassettes trying to remember names of this or that piece when suddenly, he hears Madge's voice. Like something in a dream he hears a recorded conversation between the two of them from the past.

"*Mickey, the most amazing thing has happened . . .*"

"*You're coming back?*"

"*More amazing than that!*"

He'd screwed up the answering machine cassette and had used a music cassette instead for a while, and then had gone back to recording music on it. But while it was on the telephone, if you didn't pick up fast enough it clicked on and recorded your conversation—which is why he now hears a two-year-old conversation between separated lovers.

It is stuck between a fragment of a Beethoven Quartet and an early Dave Brubeck. Madge had called him from L.A. telling him of her triumph: the music for a documentary on the fall of Communism in Eastern Europe—the Academy Award nomination. He was telling her how proud he was and reminded her that when she'd walked out in rage and panic she'd left a new pair of shoes—he knew how much she loved shoes, her one expensive vice—some musicians had cocaine, she had shoes, he told her. And then she was giggling in pride and teary at their separation and wanting to give it another try. Their voices sounded so much younger, so eager, self-satisfied. If they'd had children they might have sounded like this.

Mickey is charged up with hope and coffee. He hits rewind and cues up the tape to the start of the voices. Then he dials the number for Madge's sister hoping that she is away and thus he will not run into interference. Madge answers, wide awake before six A.M.

"Madge," he says. "Good morning. This is Michael."

"No, it's not," she says. "It's just Mickey. I'd know you anywhere."

"How are you?"

"Wide awake. I'm still on New York time."

"Hey," he says, "listen."

He hits the play button, holds the cassette player to the telephone. The conversation unreels: achievement, pride, luck, reconciliation.

"My God," she breathes. "How—?"

"Two years ago. I was using a music cassette for the answering machine and you called—"

"With the news about the nomination. Listen how excited I was. This is weird, hearing it now."

He clicks the machine off and chances his confession. "Then I forgot about our being recorded and I used the tape for more music."

She is quiet. Then: "Mickey—play that back again, would you?"

He does so, exquisitely careful to avoid a note of music on either side of the talk. It is safer to replay the tape than to keep explaining.

For the moment, Madge seems like a child listening to a story about her parents' past life, ready to hear it over and over again, talking in between, then asking to hear it again, again. For the moment she appears to have forgotten about her father, about General de Gaulle, about dogs in beds and the orderly processions of weddings. Mickey holds his breath, hoping that this haphazard capture of a moment when success and happiness seemed to be the same thing will replace Madge's resentment and confusion, make the happiness of the past seem possible. Sure enough she starts to laugh.

The two of them stay on the phone, caught between fast forward and rewind, between California and New York, between independence and love, between order and chaos, laughing and listening, listening and laughing for a long, long time—longer than either one of them had ever planned.

Messenger

She told him she'd known Max Messenger in New York and London. Singer wasn't sure how much the young woman knew about his own complicated friendship with Max. The question didn't come up in any detail until she was well ensconced; it rose to the surface in the second day of what was to have been a brief stopover on the way to Orvieto.

She'd waltzed in, all eagerness and innocence, to Prezio—the ugly, cheap little hilltop Italian town that was his refuge from the disappointments of recent years. As much as Singer didn't want any intrusion into his hiding place, there was no way he could have said "don't come"; she'd told him she'd been his daughter's art teacher in Geneva, and once Jessica's name had been spoken there was no turning back. She might bring news of a silent, angry, alienated Jessica; or she might present a Jessica ready to forget, perhaps even to forgive.

Of course the expression "waltzed in" hardly describes the grit and determination it must have taken for this young woman to get to him. Prezio was only a few miles from the autostrada, but those few miles were unpaved. *Bruta!* When he'd arrived the workmen leaned on their shovels, shook their heads in disgust as if to say the roads were rocky disasters, that he should turn back, go and stay somewhere else.

If it had been tough for him, how hellish an approach must it have been for this determined young woman. The reasons she gave at first to explain her arrival were murky; she was on her way to Orvieto, which was only a half hour away if you took the autostrada, and she'd heard so much about him. Not a word about having seen any of his work, or who *she* really was: a teacher, a painter, a critic, a groupie. Only Max and Jessica's names were extended as slender threads between them, like bank references for someone asking for a loan. She'd sounded so serious on the phone, a flat, straight voice, a schoolteacher, spinster voice. In the flesh, however, Maggie was a beauty; slender, long aristocratic neck, distracted hazel eyes flitting everywhere, wispy ash-blonde hair which she tossed every few minutes as if she were afraid she'd lose his attention if she did not, and long slender legs. Only a man who'd been without female company for so long would make such a thorough inventory.

"I can't believe I'm really here," she said. She gazed around the drab, barely furnished farmhouse, comfortless and grim.

"Neither can I." The dryness seemed to be lost on her. "And, as you can see, there's not much 'here' here."

"Jessica warned me. She said you were in your minimalist period."

"Did she mean life or art? I'm not doing much painting, money is tight, and my neck is tight from lying on my back delicately daubing a four-hundred-year-old church ceiling. Right now restoration is my game."

"I think she meant everything at once. She's good at that."

"She's not very good at calling her old man."

"Maybe that's because he's not an old man."

Was she flirting? Did young people flirt any more? Singer was not yet forty-five but sometimes among the very young he felt like an anthropologist taking notes about a strange tribe: primitive but sophisticated. It was hard to sort out.

"How old are you?" he asked.

"Ah, old enough to fight my way across Italy. I'm starved. You wouldn't have a cup of something would you?"

It seemed to seal a welcome but if he couldn't throw her out, he might as well give her tea. "This tea is wonderful. I got a taste for tea in London."

"How long have you lived in England?"

"I don't know that I've *lived* anywhere. Except for the years when I taught at Haversham in Connecticut. Where I met Jessica; a gift."

He noticed she'd not told him how old she was. She could have been anywhere from twenty-six to thirty-two. She crossed and uncrossed very long legs.

She said, "You seem to have lost a lot—or rather given up a lot."

He responded with caution, but there was something about her that pulled at the edges of his reticence and he ended up telling her a bit too much, more quickly than he liked. He'd been alone, too long; except for his one Italian friend, Mario Carelli.

"This part of my life is for hiding out. All I've given up—*if* I've given it up—is that New York scramble."

He did not mention that his last show had been a disaster, worse than invisible. No sales, zero reviews.

"Oh, it's not so bad here," Singer said, cool, controlled. "It's as if I'd had the flu and I'm convalescing. I still have my rent-controlled loft in Soho, my safety net." She sipped her tea so slowly, Singer expected something portentous when she finally spoke.

"Are you convalescing from Max Messenger's death?"

"Actually, no," he said quickly. "We fell out some time before that." It was the first real clue to why she was here. Was she one of

Max's "widows," one of the long string of brief or extended affairs—
one that might be extending beyond death? Max and Singer had been
the closest and strangest of friends in a life only they knew.

There was no way he would allow this seductive, aggressive
young woman into that secret life. *"Are you convalescing after Max
Messenger's death?"* For Christ's sake, was she trying to make *him* one
of Max's widows?

She used only the formal full name, Max Messenger, as if to make
it clear that she had not been one of the endless train of lovers, midnight encounters, one-night stands; a predatory sexual style of life
that had begun in high school, maybe earlier, then on into the Hans
Hoffman Studio School in Provincetown, and continued nonstop,
in his thirties and forties, when he was becoming a minor cult figure
all over Europe. It had ended only with his death in London, six
months ago.

Max with his trademark half-serious, half-joking manner had
once said: "Do I detect a touch of envy? Big mistake. Just think of me
as a man who needs a day nurse and a night nurse." Had she been a
day nurse or a night nurse, this Maggie?—she was just Maggie, no
last name offered.

Jessica had told her that Singer was Max Messenger's only childhood friend, his only lifelong friend. Whoever Maggie was, whatever
her mission, he couldn't toss her out after the *bruta* journey—her
shapely jaw slack with fatigue, her car battered and bruised, the windshield wiper not working so well, the tires looking thirsty for more
air. So he gave her the guest room downstairs, the one with the low
beamed ceiling, set her up with a few towels and took her to lunch in
Orvieto, a half-hour on the smooth autostrada in his borrowed four-
wheel-drive jeep.

"This is so nice of you, it's beautiful here."

It was indeed. The square surrounding the *duomo* in Orvieto was a marvelous melding of antiquity, scaffolding and exterior renovations, with a smattering of gift shops. The alleyways through which they'd made their way had been a source of delight for Maggie. As was Giglio's, the small but dependable restaurant exactly across from the cathedral. And even the gift shops and the stream of tourists clicking their cameras couldn't foul up that amazing bristling but elegant *duomo*.

"Why did you choose Italy for your hideout?"

"I won the Prix de Rome right out of Columbia—a year—and Italy got into my blood." He let the vodka talk for a moment. "When my career and what we laughingly call my life hit a new low, I figured I'd come back to the country where I had my biggest high."

She was tactful enough to move on—she would not allow him to embarrass himself. Singer appreciated this but thought, also, she's a smooth one.

"Are you doing any of your own painting?"

It was a politeness and Singer treated it as such, no more.

But over her vermouth and his second vodka he came out with it.

He focused his eyes on those long, contoured legs, not on her face; it was easier when you were going to say something unpleasant.

"You've made a hell of a trip to see me. But it's about Max isn't it? What is it you want?"

"People always assume people want something."

"Neither of us is just 'people.' You know Jessica; you were her teacher. What did she tell you about me and Max? And what's in it for you?"

She leaned back in her chair and performed her leg-crossing number again. "So many questions. Can't you at least put them in some kind of order? And can't they wait till *we* order? I'm starved." She rustled her menu and waved it at him.

"Whatever you need from me, you won't get it by playing boy-girl games."

"Why? Is there some dark-eyed Italian wench lurking around a corner?"

"Even Italy doesn't have wenches any more, Maggie. I recommend the veal."

She shook her head, suddenly very determined. "Not veal. Do you know how they keep the calves—?"

"Then the pastas are terrific here. And they're not hurt in the cooking process."

But over the Linguine Bolognese she was persistent. "Isn't it lonely, doesn't it feel odd to be out of the 'scramble' as you called it?" It was better, he told her, for him now to forget about the future and take his hand to the past. He gave her a glimpse of where he was, but a safe quick look; told her there was a strange kind of exhilaration in lying on a scaffolding, a mock touching-up Leonardo, with a perpetual crick in his neck, working in carefully prescribed formats of restoration. Like painting-by-numbers; freed for once from that desperate itch to make something that had never existed before, an itch he and Max had suffered from all their young lives. This was different: don't make it new, just get it back to what it was supposed to be. Of course there were nuances, probably a little like translating poetry; something of the restorer's hand seeped in. That notion helped, especially some nights after a glass or two of wine, alone in the big, grimy house in Prezio.

But it took genuine control to keep Max out of it. There was one fresco that was supposed to contain a cartoon by Raphael—though it was not authenticated; Singer consoled himself by thinking of the broad cartoons of his last few years; the political paintings which had given him such pleasure to make and which had only widened the gulf between him and Max. Giant fresco-like paintings of a gun pointed at an artist's head; an electric chair, heavily outlined and shadowed, made to seem so grand and terrifying, it was like a negative holy icon.

"Op Ed Page Art," Messenger had said.

"Borromeo used to put his political enemies in ridiculous positions—like Dante," Singer had said in his own defense. Max was a hungry reader and he'd replied, "There's Dante the killer-judge and there's Dante the poet. You're playing a tricky game here." Max had lit the usual new cigarette from the usual old cigarette, and from a cloud of smoke continued, "Besides, if you're going to play Dante you'll need a guide, a Virgil."

"That would be you."

Max did his smoke-squint, shook his head and said, "Don't count on me. Judging doesn't interest me. I just care about the poetry. Politics is shit!"

To Max, politics was a one-way ticket to nowhere, a dead-end for anybody serious. When Philip Guston gave up his shimmering abstract canvases for political cartoon-paintings, Max's obvious disgust should have warned him how Max would react when Singer moved in the same direction. It would be the first overt crack in a solid wall of cameraderie.

That part was the stuff he didn't tell her.

Maggie sipped her wine and persisted. "Does it pay enough, this restoration work?"

Singer laughed; it had been a while since he'd laughed out loud.

"Pays so well that I have to teach a class in what we used to call 'art appreciation' twice a week just to make the rent. And, to complicate things, I'm an illegal. My friend Mario did a little underhand helping on the sly. They don't like foreigners teaching art in Italy."

"I'd love to sit in one night."

"Something tells me you already appreciate art—maybe a little too much."

It was the closest he had come to letting Max creep into the discourse.

He called Mario Carelli, who'd gotten him the job and who supervised the project; told him he needed a few days off. The work was sporadic, in any case, and Mario was a fan of Singer's political paintings—failures in America but the Italians have a tenderness for anything of the political left. Mario worked around Singer's absences. There followed two days of some rather stiff, awkward sightseeing. He had told himself that he couldn't just throw her out after her difficult trek. But was that just his excuse for a lingering curiosity, for a loneliness he hadn't admitted to himself? It was complicated. He didn't trust her and didn't know how to get rid of her. She seemed to sense this, and, in a pinch, would introduce small anecdotes about Jessica—Singer was hungry for inside information about his daughter, her letters were few and uninformative; there was no way to tell if any healing of their rift had set in.

To break the ice he told Maggie as much as he thought he needed, and as little as he could.

He told her what she, perhaps, already knew something of. Jessica had been his darling, the one remnant of an awful marriage to a promiscuous young woman of an aristocratic British family—a duchess or a countess, he could never get straight who was lying about lineage and who was not. The titles were all a shambles, and the whole gang was full of airs but broke. About his wife's uncontrollable roaming, Singer used to console himself with Browning's lines: *She had / A heart—how shall I say?—too soon made glad, / Too easily impressed; she liked whate'er / She looked on, and her looks went everywhere.*

Singer, on his part, was congenitally monogamous, according to Christina.

"Congenital," he'd said. "You make it sound like a kind of inherited disease."

"I'm just trying to excuse my own bad behavior, darling. Or should I say 'bed' behavior? Clearly, I'm the one who's inherited the problem. My mother led my old man a merry chase." Singer had salvaged nothing from the marriage but Jessica, gaining custody with hardly a struggle. After Christina was gone, Max Messenger became

Jessica's surrogate "mother": art galleries on weekdays, museums on Sundays. Mercurial with everyone else, he was steadfast with this bright-eyed child, from third grade to the beginning of high school. Max was solo by then, had been married twice, no children of his own; his paintings, his collages, his outer-edge photographs—he called them his babies, not hesitating at infanticide if one didn't turn out well. But Jessica was the precious child, an emblem of the children Max didn't have or really want for himself. "Look at how Charlie Chaplin's kids turned out; look at Thomas Mann's kids or Picasso's—not for me. Children of great men don't do well." He was half-grinning to hide behind the joking comparisons—but Max knew where he stood. The three M's of the twentieth century: Mondrian, Magritte, Messenger. He had placed himself while still in high school, long before the official placers had begun. And, as Singer's closest comrade, Max took up the task of introducing his best friend's daughter into the mysteries of paint and paper, of visual images and the spirit of looking. But that was before Singer and Max began to confuse friendship with envy, achievement with sexual aggressions, all of it crying out for some kind of revenge; on whom and for what was never quite clear.

And now here was this reminder of the distant and all-too-recent past, intruding into his spare, deliberately isolated present, the present of an eccentric American painter now on something of a descent of his own; no longer doing his own work, keeping body and soul together by restoring frescoes—not in the grand cathedral—in Orvieto; not Pieros, just Leonettis, a less celebrated, less original painter whose years of birth and death were identical with those of the the greater artist; time-darkened frescoes in a tiny time-darkened church near the summit of Orvieto. *Are you convalescing from Max Messenger's death?* Not such a dumb question. It had only been six months. And Singer's flight to Italy coincided a little too neatly with his stock-taking and his decision to try a new life—to try to live *without* a life.

As if in exchange Maggie tossed some tidbits about Jessica—how good she had become at soccer, how serious she was about art history; about a boy named Peter; how she'd cheated on a test and then admitted it to Maggie, tore it up and asked for a replay with a different test.

"Like her father," Singer said. "Gives in to temptation and then regrets it."

Was he flirting, now, or what passed for it at his age? He hadn't slept with a woman in almost a year. Sensing trouble in himself as well as her, he wanted to stay in control, he would carefully count the glasses of wine at dinner, two at the most.

He walked her through the elegant little Church of San Giovanni on the upward sloping street near the top of Orvieto, showed her the frescoes he was working on, enormous ones: yet another Last Judgment.

"I thought only Italians were allowed to do restoration."

"It's a temporary permit. But you should see the paperwork."

"And does all this leave time to do any of your own painting?"

He tossed her a savage smile. "I'm getting hungry; how about you?"

They walked down the Via Garibaldi to a little trattoria for dinner and Singer was preparing to ask her to leave, though he had not yet organized the right words. As if to nerve himself for taking control, he ordered for her: "You'll like the quail here, local, very tender."

Maggie looked pale, tired.

"I think we may have walked you around a little too much today."

She smiled at him over the wine list. "You keep ordering wine by the glass, and it's not so great. Could we maybe have a bottle of this terrific-looking Barolo?"

Over his second glass of this terrific Barolo he decided: either he would learn what Max had to do with all this, or just tell her that he had to get back to his own painting in the little shed behind the house that passed for a studio, that the mysterious little visit was over.

"What's whipping you around the globe like this? London, New York, California, Orvieto, Prezio . . . ?"

"A project," she said. "Have another glass of wine. I didn't tell you but I'm something of a fan of yours, too."

He wasn't crazy about the "too" and he felt foolish for wanting to hear more. It was a long time between drinks and he was thirsty.

It turned out she meant his late pieces; the electric chair series, the gun paintings. "They were powerful, scary."

"Yeah," he said mournfully, in spite of himself, "I was scary for a while."

Later he could not believe that he'd allowed her to get him drunk, that she was in charge, that seduction was in her hands.

"The project," she said, leaning forward to secure and hold his gaze and his attention, "is a book."

"About Max?"

"About Max." She paused and let him have the full force of the emotion that had been in hiding. "I think he's one of the greatest painters we've had."

Now it was "we've" had. She had his attention, she had the hairs on the back of his neck crawling.

"And that's why you made this trek?"

"I've got a contract and an advance. In fact, I'll pay for this Barolo, if you'll finish the bottle with me and loosen up enough to talk to me about him."

"What kind of stuff do you want to know?"

"Well, I've spoken to a lot of people: Jerry Greenberg, George Lowry, Sarah Sesch, Jean Larkin, Maureen—well, to a lot of women."

"I'll bet." He sniffed and drank, sniffed and drank. The Barolo was aromatic, what you might call a thoughtful wine. Or at least that's the kind of notion that crossed your mind when more than half the bottle was gone and you were trying to dance around questions that were memories and memories that were questions. Also, it was eighteen years old; he was not used to drinking wine that had been bottled before he came to Italy.

She was intent now, no jokes, no flirting. "You were his oldest friend. Well, earliest, I mean. You knew Max in high school, didn't you? What was he like as a youngster?"

"He was a black sheep even then. In drawing class he used to deliberately draw his own partially rubbed out version of what the teacher, Mr. Marione, wanted us to do. Then, on the one occasion— this was a famous story around school—we were allowed to sketch a female nude from life and Max went behind the screen where the model was putting her clothes back on and asked her if she wanted to make a little extra money."

Maggie was scribbling madly in a notebook. She paused and pulled out a tiny tape recorder she'd secreted in her bag. "Hold up," Singer said. "I haven't decided to do this."

Her tongue moistened the corners of her mouth. "Yes, you have," she said.

"Besides, I can't believe you want crap like that in your book."

"Every detail," she said. "Do you know how famous Max has become since he died? There's a newsletter out of Berlin and one out of Los Angeles; there's a TV documentary starting up for the BBC. And Web sites—"

"And books," he said. "How many books?"

"I think I'm the first." She tossed off the last half glass and said, looking quite different, fierce, "I'd damned well better be the first."

He wanted to ask her if this was ambition or posthumous love; if she was one of the widows, or if this was the genuine article; loving what Max had done in his later squeezed-down work and being driven to celebrate it. But by now he was woozy and all he could say was, "Is this going to be a Life or a Life and Works?"

"Both," she said and he asked her to drive them back as he was now too drunk to drive and she seemed stone cold and he would guide her, very carefully, very slowly, over the *bruta* roads.

In the morning Singer had a headache, slept, woke, slept again and woke nauseated and hungry as hell. But he was nervous about going downstairs and facing her. She was fresh, snappy, and already cooking a large breakfast. "Good morning," she said. "Ready to go?"

He wasn't ready for anything except for cup after cup of coffee. Over her bacon and eggs she said, "Anything, don't censor, small or large, everything counts."

"Didn't your mother tell you never to talk with your mouth full? You know I haven't done any work in the church or my studio since you appeared out of the blue." He thought he might divert her attention to himself, but she was implacable. "His favorite writers for example."

"Well, Kafka certainly."

Her smile had a tinge of reminiscence.

"No," Singer said. "Not that Kafka, not the mysterious trials or castles. His favorite quote was, 'Life being what it is one dreams of revenge.' "

Once, during a lunch break at San Giovanni, Singer had asked Mario Carelli if he knew the Kafka quote. "No," Mario said, "but in Italy we have a saying, 'Revenge is a dish best tasted cold.' "

"I forgot," Singer said. "This is the home of opera."

Mario had tossed him an innocent, dark-eyed gaze. "Revenge is in all our books, our music; revenge is in the air you breathe in Italy. Dante is our prophet and all these Last Judgments are a kind of revenge of God's."

Singer had not expected such an aria on the theme.

"In fact," Mario said between bites of a gigantic hero sandwich, "people who wouldn't dream of an act of revenge anywhere else find it much easier in Italy." He embarked on a long, complicated story involving his sister-in-law and a visiting Frenchman; but Singer had tuned out, taken entirely by the idea of the patience of making a cold dish out of hot revenge.

"Life being what it is—" Maggie murmured. "When was he reading things like Kafka? I mean what period of his life, high school? Afterwards when he was living on Bleeker Street? Was he married yet?"

His hunger returned and he turned away from her towards the eggs and bacon. Over his shoulder he said, "Listen, I was not Boswell to his Johnson. I didn't go around taking notes on Max." He turned back and drilled her a stare. "In those days, don't forget, it wasn't clear who was going to come out ahead, me, him, Paul Resicka, Wolf Kahn, Larry Rivers . . . It was the steeplechase of youth. Max hadn't pulled so far ahead yet. It took death to arrange that."

She seemed immune to any overtone of bitterness, loaded for bear. "Did he ever alternate between abstract and the figure? Did he show any interest in installation art in the early days? Where did you first meet him? How close were you in high school?"

"Jesus, okay—one: sometimes; two: no; three: in the studio class; and four: very. Now can you make any sense of that?"

"Absolutely." She was triumphant. This was a skirmish and she sensed she'd won. "He sometimes painted the figure, sometimes not, he showed no interest in installation art, you met him when you both hung out in school and you were very close then." She finished scribbling. "I'm going to be good at this," she said. "Now, can I turn it on?" Singer saw that the tape recorder had been sitting, menacing, at the edge of the table as if it was poised to fall off or to be turned on, final, irrevocable.

"Okay," Singer said, thinking: a temporary surrender. He would find a way to avoid total defeat. At the back of his mind without allowing full remembrance, he knew there was, of course, at least one small secret he would never introduce, a foolish, even childish but painful, secret resentment.

His temporary surrender, as he thought of it during the next few days, eased her a bit; she became alternately flirtatious and charming, warmly grateful but always persistent. The weather too seemed to respond, the heat eased and the skies became Italian blue. A cool breeze followed Maggie and Singer on long walks down vistas framed by tall pines. They would stop only at the imperious demand of the tape recorder. After a while it seemed to him as if he was mainly talking about his own life, which of course he was; there was no separating his life from Max's.

One evening, after Maggie had done a pasta and chicken for dinner with more Barolo, he even dug out an essay he had written, a catalogue piece for one of Max's early shows. It was full of the warmth of early, easy friendship, not yet haunted by the specter of discipleship, or competitiveness. Max and Singer were tied together, too, by a mutual love of literary history—Max had read everything and, in those days, his art was full of literary references. Kafka, of course, and Celine, and Artaud—artists of the cruel.

She asked if she could keep the essay and Singer gave it to her. She had been smiling but now the smiles stopped and she folded the piece away among the other written notes for her project. She kissed him on the cheek by way of thanks; had her lips lingered a little long on his cheek? Or was he just dulled with wine and the false domesticity, the long-ago lost pleasures of conventionality, of a woman cooking dinner and conversing of an evening? He felt instantly foolish and went to bed abruptly, leaving her with her notes and tapes.

It was all somehow different after that. Maggie was still absolutely intent on her mission; they were still playing the ping-pong game of question and answer, of memory and revelation. But now for Singer it was a *different* game. It was amusing to him that a kiss on the cheek should turn him upside down. He determined to hurry things along, to set a time limit, maybe two more days.

Maggie got it, she was tuned in. Her questioning became even more direct. Singer's anecdotes became more openly sexual, as with Max they naturally must, rarely without laughter. The next afternoon she said, "I have some homework for you."

"Oh?"

"I want you to write down any central incident of the time you were hanging around together, the earlier the better."

"Why?

They were sitting in the back of the house, on what passed for a backyard patio, trying to avoid the sun by shielding in shadows, alternately swatting flies and sipping iced tea. She gave him one of those ambiguous stares she was so good at and said, "Because there's something inside there that I'm not getting. Something that maybe went wrong."

"Are you training to be a psychoanalyst?" In a second he was furious, as much with himself as with her, with the whole situation he'd allowed himself to be sucked into. "Who the hell are you?" He stood up and hovered over her, not loomed as Max would have done, a combination of power and seductiveness, just angry, helpless, hovering. "What are you going to do for the rest of your life? You can't live forever on a book about Max Messenger. I don't know a damn thing about you and here you're poking—"

"You haven't asked. Not really, anyway. It's not so mysterious. I'm a child of the seventies. I drifted into advertising art, was a pretty good designer; in the go-go art world of the eighties I taught, art and art history, no advanced degree, so it had to be a private school like Haversham, which, of course is where I met Jessica. What more do you want to know?" She was getting angry, too. "Did I sleep with Max? What sounds do I make when I come, did I love him, did he love me?"

She forced an artificial calm by turning away to swat away a persistent fly. "I think maybe you're afraid to tell me why the two of you drifted apart after having been, what, such close buddies?"

Singer had to laugh, remembering fifteen years of orbiting each other. "Buddies? There was hardly a day in fifteen years that we didn't see each other—if it got too late it was assumed that one or the other of us would bed down on a couch and stay over. The talk was phenomenal. Max was one of the great talkers."

In a quick swipe she had the tape on again. "What'd you talk about?"

"What didn't we talk about! Art, the downtown scene, the uptown scene, rascally literature like Diderot's *Rameau's Nephew*, Genet, Nietzsche, communists, anarchists—Max was born to admire rebellion, betrayal, all forms of the unexpected. We hung out with other crazies, too—Larry Krebs, Jack Morris; when Edgar Varese came to America, we were the first in line at the concert; when Max Frisch lectured at Columbia, Max—my Max—managed to weasel out where he was staying and trapped him in the elevator of this apartment building on the upper west side and grilled him about what was happening in German art and German writing. The three of us ended up getting drunk at the West End bar."

Singer realized that, in some clownish way, he had gone from rage to rhapsodic. Had he really called him "my Max"? But he couldn't stop; a gate had been opened and it wouldn't be closed until he could lock Maggie out or in.

He was up and pacing, now, as if dictating his memoirs. "It was a daily feast of being young and drunk on art; when I had my first one-man show at a tiny gallery on East 72nd Street—a bunch of conventional imitations of de Kooning, some of Franz Kline, just for variety—Max asked me, 'Will this change the way we look at things?' It was the first hint of the trouble."

Maggie was alert. "Yes, the trouble. Would that be the central incident I asked you to write down before you went ape on me?"

"There wasn't any one incident," he lied. "But this was the first moment that I got the idea—Max wanted to be on the cutting edge of Art and I was just delighted at getting something on a wall. He was the avant-garde, I was the bourgeois. We ended up, Max with his loft on Bleeker Street and me in a basement apartment on 74th and Lexington. You can figure it by art or by real estate."

There wasn't any one incident. The lie is naturally about something sexual. A precursor of the suppression of the big lie; but there was time for that; there might always be time for that. Out of the blue, but with all the force of a suppressed memory, Judy Kapell springs to mind. Darkly Jewish, adolescent worker for Zionist causes, wearer of unfashionable but dashing, long, ground-sweeping skirts, seventeen to Singer's and Max's sixteen; the seemingly unattainable Judy Kapell who haunted that spring term, Judy Kapell of the first loss of innocence, of trust. Of necessity, Singer had to abort the surge of memory. Had Maggie read his mind? Was there something so strong about the return of an early love, so full of mysterious magic that its betrayal could be sensed by anyone? How the hell had she known that there was one incident, hidden, one incident, trivial compared to the long ideological, the long psychological rift between old friends; one foolish buried bitterness, buried perhaps because so foolish, so old. Still, it was the threat of rage that made him cut short the evening and head for bed. *Life being what it is one dreams of revenge.* A high school Count of Monte Cristo. Singer could bear no more. He left a surprised Maggie behind, bewildered; one small satisfaction.

He lay awake, exhausted by fighting off black flies, by fighting off Maggie, by fighting off poisonous memories. Alone in the enormous bed the landlord had provided for him—suddenly it felt too big; before Maggie's arrival it had felt pleasantly spacious. He tried to listen to the unfamiliar birdsong; apparently bird cries were as national as people. But he was also listening to fragments of his unfinished dialogue with Max Messenger, a colloquy he'd thought was finished. Maggie had brought it to life again and now it wouldn't go away.

Max: "You're so fucking serious. Even about fucking. Until you get to the play part in art, you'll never be really serious." All stuff he couldn't or wouldn't tell Maggie. Maggie, the emptiness of the great bed and the image of her best feature, her long legs, all mixed together as he dozed off at last.

Singer was not a late sleeper. But the combination of unaccustomed wine-drinking and the pressure of Maggie's persistence helped him sleep the morning and a piece of the afternoon away. Even after waking, he lay long in bed, as if gathering his forces for a showdown. Two days, he had decided after last night's sudden flight, two days and then *finito*.

He lay long also nursing a queasy stomach and a headache. Never, he vowed, drink old wine with young women. At last he turned over and glanced at the bedside clock. It was two-thirty in the afternoon. By the time he'd showered and dressed, it was already three o'clock.

Maggie was in the kitchen. "*Buon giorno,*" she said. "A handy phrase. It doesn't specify morning or afternoon. Just 'good day.' "

Singer grinned weakly and she said, "What'll it be, breakfast or lunch?"

"I think all I can handle might be a soldier's breakfast: coffee and a cigarette. Except I've sworn off cigarettes years ago."

"Me, too," Maggie said. "Coffee it is." She looked so at home now, wearing shorts and a T-shirt, pouring coffee for both of them. They were in danger of becoming an old, feuding couple, familiar, wary.

It was all very convivial until Singer said, "Maggie, this has to be finished in two days."

"Why two days?"

"Because I want you to get out the tape recorder and I'll stop hedging. I'll tell you what I know and you'll be on your way. It's been an unusual experience, but I have to get on with my life. Two days: maximum!"

Startled into silence, she obeyed: tape set up, questions on her tongue. But Singer was not to be passive anymore.

"We'll start with the big question: why did Max and I drift away? Then there are three scenes I'll play for you—and something I have to show you."

She was quiet, compelled by his new manner which was at once cooperative and dismissive. She seemed almost chagrined; about to get what she had come all this way for, but under some shadow of disappointment; as if what she wanted had changed, as if being tossed out in two days full of the information she'd come for was a kind of defeat not a victory.

"It started gradually . . ."

"What's *it* . . ."

Singer held up his hand like a traffic cop. "Please." And continued: "There was no one big humiliation scene. This is life not opera. But little by little, the circle of his friends grew bigger, jazzier, bigger names in painting, music, even writing—all an outer edge crowd, by now it was international. At first he took me in with him—to the openings, to the interviews. But gradually I would find myself left out or worse, standing with the disciples he was gathering. I was changing roles; closest friend becomes Peter or Paul or, worst of all, Thomas." Singer was in opera, now, singing an aria of rage and resentment, feeling as wounded as if it had all just happened.

"Finally, there *was* an incident. Max had gotten so distracted by his new life that he gave a talk to a packed house at Cooper Union. One of his nonlinear, e.e.cummings kind of talks about the art scene—I knew it because he'd tried it out on me days before. When I got to Cooper Union there was a line around the block and Max hadn't left a ticket for me."

Singer could tell how whiny he sounded. It made him pause.

Maggie took advantage of the pause by standing up, suddenly, those supple legs flashing at Singer as her robe parted and closed again. She said, simply, "Perhaps he forgot." She moved closer to him, waiting for a storm to pass or erupt.

"No," Singer said, "it was the little gods who rule over success and failure who forgot . . . favoring one, forgetting another, oh, Jesus, I hate this self-pity and I've kept it under lock and key until you showed up and opened all this shit. The trouble isn't that I wasn't cut out to be a disciple—the trouble is, I *was*, I *am* and that's why I hated it so. I wanted my friend back, the way it was when we hung out together on the fringe of the future. The Cooper Union thing happened a week after I'd sent him the sketches for an Art Book—an experiment on Wallace Stevens—in the old days we showed each other everything we did and he lost the sketches and forgot to tell me . . ."

As it happened they were color xeroxes but Singer didn't want to tell her that; if he was going to binge on past resentments, then he would binge. "I thought we would be, you know, first among equals, isn't that how it goes? I'm not dumb enough to think it was just those two things. It was building for a long time and I know that Max knew but he had a sort of gruff detachment by this time, maybe just embarrassed, I don't know which would be worse. For God's sake, *I was waiting in line in our lives and I didn't even have a ticket.*"

He was on the verge of something, tears perhaps, and Maggie took advantage of the moment by pressing her cheek against his, as if to see if it was wet or dry. Singer turned his face to her so that their lips were an inch apart, ready for the unthinkable. How to hold it off, because it must be held off, for reasons entirely genuine but still mysterious. What would be so awful about a little comfort in his harsh life, would it be so awful to fill that too-big bed upstairs with Maggie's clinging body? It was just that until Singer got certain things cleared away he felt vulnerable, in danger. He turned his back to her, running events, memories, angers through his mind; he still had the need to tell her, to involve her in the foolish rages, mistakes, missteps. No! He would not tell her about the early betrayal: Judy Kapell, so silly in recollection that Singer was reluctant to fish it out. It was so much more trivial than the other betrayal, not long before Max died.

He turned back having narrowly avoided the extra humiliation of tears. Singer forced a grin. "Well," he said, "enough of the dark stuff, let me give you the second scene, something a little lighter and brighter, though it has a dark ending."

She forced a smile in return. "I'll take anything. My tape recorder is neutral, open for anything. Let's sit down. Coffee and confessions."

He obeyed; his experiment had gone off the tracks; the control seemed somehow to have shifted to Maggie.

Singer sipped and sang his sad song. "Max was no dope—to say the least. He knew what was happening to us. And not long after, he tried some healing. The next time he had a show, he called me; it was a little awkward, but we got through it, probably because we both knew what was at stake.

"I got there late, I guess because I was nervous. People were standing around in the usual clusters, wineglasses in hand. Then, conventional asshole that I was—still am—I expected him to clear the slate."

"An apology?"

"Listen, Maggie, I can barely do this at all, but if you make it a dialogue I'm finished. I'm doing this in the morning because I didn't want to make it go down easier with Barolo, a perfect excuse."

"I'll shut up."

"I doubt that, but anyway what Max did then was to take a medium-sized piece off the wall—I think the paint was still a little wet—took a brush he'd prepared and painted, small and elegant but clear so you could read it, 'To my friend Simon Singer, with all my love and admiration.'"

Maggie of course, could not shut up at this. "You own a Messenger?" It was the first time she'd used his last name alone, the art-historical name.

But Singer was too wrung out for amusement, for irony. He had watched her noting his grim surroundings, the house full of flies, the impassable roads. She might be converting the Messenger into hard cash, in her head.

He kept going, couldn't stop now if he wanted to. "I was too stuffed with self-pity to let the gesture, the gift, the inscription work the way I think Max intended it to: a healing . . . I missed the moment. Thanked him, left with my neatly wrapped prize and let the downward drift keep on until finally there was so much space between us that building a bridge was hopeless; beyond my engineering skills."

Singer had almost forgotten Maggie was there. The remorse-moment was his, alone; she entered it, stared. He stared back; she stood up and moved towards him again. In this game of cat and cat she was on her feet and standing close to him; long, lissome, driven by engines of ambition, with a natural talent for mockery and for spelunking into the caves of others; her closeness pulled some suspicion out of him he hadn't known was there. He grasped her, holding her at arm's length, and said:

"You weren't Jessica's teacher at all, were you." It was not a question and her embarrassed smile was her answer, even before she said, "I met her at a party in Soho. I saw a way to use her as a cover story when I finally tracked you down. Don't be mad, please."

Singer surprised himself with the kiss; a small sensual aggression, a change of command. He'd been feeling hunted, now he was the hunter. He was not quite sure what he would do next, but he knew that the kiss was something he had to do. Her lips tasted dry, familiar, not like a first kiss.

The problem of what to do next was quickly solved by the sound of a four-wheel drive Fiat pickup truck.

"Oh, Christ," Singer said, "I forgot—I have a class, today at six o'clock. And I missed one last week, but I promised Mario only one time out. You've distracted me, Maggie."

"I'll pay the difference," she said.

"No thanks. I'll do the class."

Singer bustled around giving Mario Carelli coffee and apologies.

"We've missed you," Mario said. "I've read up on the Abstract Art of the Fifties and early Sixties, Pop Art of the Seventies, I'm all ready for tonight—the Eighties."

Hearing Mario now, it all sounded jejeune, breaking up everything into decades, as if each ten years had been monolithic; but Singer had needed some structure for speaking to a group of Italians not knowing how much the small but eager class knew.

"I'm sorry, Mario, but this lady (in Italy all women were still ladies) has come a great distance to interview me. Mr. Carelli, Miss—" Suddenly Singer realized he did not know Maggie's last name. It had never come up.

"Messenger," Maggie said.

Mario said hello with a wise Italian gaze at his American teacher, with a beautiful young woman, wearing short shorts. "Messenger," he said. "Are you of the family of the painter?"

Maggie nodded avoiding Singer's astonished eyes.

Mario drained his tiny cup of bitter coffee. To Singer, he said, "Then I guess you will cancel class, today. This is now a small difficulty because my pal Dominick dropped me off. I thought I would go in your car."

Singer suddenly could not bear the idea of being alone with Maggie for one more minute. "No, we won't cancel class. Just let me get my stuff."

To Maggie, Mario said, "I don't mean to interrupt. But please come along. He is a marvelous teacher."

In the car Mario launched into a nonstop monologue on the history of Umbria, of Orvieto, of the Church of San Giovanni where the classes took place. Singer and Maggie shut down conversation, letting Mario carry the day, avoiding each other's eyes.

Walking up the long hill from the parking garage to the church and its classroom, Maggie and Singer were still mute. Everything had changed between them in the last hour. Stumbling past the potholes and the workmen pounding the enormous beds of almost unpassable stones and gravel, Mario Carelli kept up the flow of chatter. It seemed he had a cousin who taught Contemporary Art at the University in Milan, a member of the Communist Party but who loved the avant-garde, a passion which had brought him a lot of trouble with the Party and he, Mario himself, was honored to be in the presence of someone related to Max Messenger.

Finally, Singer could bear it no longer. Winded from the climb he found enough breath to say, "Mario, tell the lady what you told me about Italy and revenge."

Mario seemed to blush. "Why is everyone speaking of revenge? We are in Orvieto not in Tosca." In honor of the new mixture of painfully-come-by honest confession, the taste of her mouth on his, the taste of her lies, Singer said, "There are times when, even after a long time, revenge is in the air." Then, not wishing to embarrass his friend further, he told Maggie, "Mario says, the Italian saying is: Revenge is a dish best tasted cold."

"Does he?" she said. She was on a different planet, now, a cold, burned-out planet.

Singer was relentless. "He also says, when they're in Italy people find acts of revenge easier than elsewhere. Isn't that right, Mario?" But Mario was no dope. He was sensitized to nuance and the nuances felt ugly.

"Well," he said. "Just turn left and we're there."

It was a pleasure to teach the class again. Singer had never seen it as a pleasure, just a way to make some extra bucks. But tonight he riffed with unexpected energy on the absence of a general style, of the Downtown scene and the big money flowing to painters who'd barely cut their eye-teeth. As if to make up for the triviality of neatly slicing art into decades he shifted to the exceptions, to the graffiti artists, to the artists hooked on the figure: Phillip Pearlstein, Larry Rivers; swerving to the drug scene; carefully leaving out any mention of Max Messenger. He tried to ignore Maggie's presence at the back of the room, looking out of place in the classroom chair with the arm-extensions for writing on; she was like a visiting principal come to evaluate a teacher and at the same time like a schoolgirl who had blundered into the wrong classroom and didn't know how to leave without embarrassing herself and everyone else.

After dropping Mario off at his car, Singer found himself driving the newly discovered Maggie Messenger back in utter silence. He was not going to raise the question of the double deception, her trick about Jessica and the magic surname: right now he didn't give a damn if she was Max's sister or cousin—he stayed away from the thought that she might be Max's widow; most of all he stayed away from the kiss of anger, the kiss of relief at learning that she had not been Jessica's teacher; a relief as mysterious to Singer as the unexpected kiss itself.

While they'd been inside, the day had turned from that golden haze of Umbrian summer to a darker shade. Still silent, Maggie rolled down the window and let the cool breeze riffle her hair.

She broke the double silence. "You're smart about art. Max used to say being too smart was tricky."

"Bullshit," Singer said. "He was smart as they come. Sometimes he just liked to play the rough-and-ready primitive."

She'd given him the cue and he took it. "Okay," he said, moving past her deceptions, as if nothing unusual had happened, "do you still want to hear stuff?"

"I don't have my tape recorder," she said. "But I have a good memory. Besides," she turned on a cold smile, "I only have one more day in Prezio, according to you. But you did say there were three scenes you would sketch out for me. A lot has happened since then, but I'd still like to make it three for three."

It was starting to drizzle and she rolled the window back up.

"I'm going to tell you what happened when we were in school. You may laugh."

"That's the one thing I can promise you I won't do."

"Okay. Her name was Judy Kapell." And saying the name aloud after so many years, the memory invaded him completely and he had none of the trouble he'd anticipated in inviting Maggie into the high school days of Singer and Messenger.

Judy on the stairs, Judy lying on the rolling green slopes outside of school chewing on a blade of grass; Judy of the plump lips, flutist's lips all promise, all wit; she and Singer made each other laugh; laughter which followed them to the metal staircases between floors, dropping books so that the laughs could turn to a few quick kisses.

In the heedlessness of youth he'd shared the laughs and the memory of the kisses with Max. "Judy Kapell," Max had murmured, "I think I've seen her; tiny with slanty eyes. Maybe from an occasional Tartar rape during pogroms in Russia. Olive skin." Max seemed to register any interesting girl he saw, perhaps for present or future reference; he was already a rover, though it was a little too early to know if it was her eyes or other body parts that were under examination.

Max asked questions: What class was she in? Where did she live? At least one of the answers seemed to intrigue him. "Central Park South." His grin was oddly conspiratorial. "You're moving up." It wasn't necessary for Singer to point out that from where he and Max lived in Lower East Side tenements there was no place to go but up. He was right. Judy's father owned apartment houses in midtown Manhattan and hosted what passed for a salon in the late fifties.

They turned off the autostrada—Singer had chosen the fastest route; no desire to prolong matters. But now came the hard part, not just the road, but the story itself turned *bruta*, at least if you were the one remembering it, if you were the teenaged, overly intense kid involved his first acquaintance with betrayal. He'd told that to Max once who laughed, as only Max could, at what he thought of as unwarranted sensitivity, an inability to appreciate the randomness, the freedom from conventional morality that was the air he breathed. Betrayal was only another esthetic category, something out of Graham Greene or Harold Pinter or Picasso.

Hard part or not, it had to be gotten through. "Then, I forget exactly where and how I heard, but the word was out that Max had contacted Judy Kapell."

"And, of course, he slept with her."

"It was 'of course' to everybody except me. He was my friend Max. I couldn't believe it. So I challenged him. I actually said the words: did you sleep with her? I remember we were at the school cafeteria. It was winter and we were eating soup and crackers. Max looked at me, long, between spoonfuls, as if deciding whether to tell me or not. Then he decided to do both. He did what he did best: he made a joke out of it. He said: 'Sleep with Judy Kapell? Not a wink.' I went home, wept and collapsed onto my bed for a week."

Two strange sounds broke up Singer's self-absorbed journey into the past. One was the sudden pouring rain, driving against the windshield. The other was the sound of Maggie laughing uncontrollably. She was in a spasm. "I'm sorry . . ." She was gasping with the effort of controlling what she obviously knew was a mad thing to do after someone has revealed an early trauma complete with tears and collapse. "I'm really sorry . . . it's just that you were all kids and it's still . . . Oh, God . . ." Her eyes were wet with laugh-tears, then more shaking hysterics while she fished in her purse for a kleenex.

Singer pulled the car over to the shoulder—no, they were on one of those awful roads leading to the house and there was no true shoulder; he just drove half onto grass and half onto gravel, and cut the motor. Then he plunged out of the car, over to the passenger side and pulled Maggie out into the rain with him. He was in some kind of fury, pushed into a state he didn't recognize because it was new to him. The rain was driven by wind so that in two seconds they were both standing, soaked.

It was time for the second kiss, this time an angry one. He tumbled her, half onto grass, half onto gravel, heedless of the grotesquerie of the moment. Her skirt came up quickly, partly because she was not unwilling, seemed excited by the unexpectedness of the onslaught following her spasm of laughter which seemed to call for another spasm, this time shared.

In seconds Maggie took charge; somewhere in his fevered feelings of the moment Singer sensed that she was picking up on this weird rain-soaked coupling as his parody version of revenge and she was not going to let him have it, not going to be the victim, the stand-in for a dead friend. She rolled over and sat on him, leaning forward to push him deeper into her. His back was rubbing against sharp gravel, rocks and wet, slimy grass. He liked her riding him; he could relinquish responsibility for all of it, could black out all of the unanswered questions. What had begun as an angry way of making her answer for all the confusions of the week had now apparently turned to making love, at least for her, at least for the moment.

Afterwards they lay side by side, her eyes closed, his open. Neither of them seemed to notice that the rain had stopped; as if the storm had been timed to their storm.

"Hey," he said.

Her eyes opened; the frenzy finished, her gaze uncertain, asking what was to come next. Which turned out to be a great, roaring clap of laughter from Singer, involuntary, like a sneeze or an orgasm, shaking him so that Maggie, her arms still around him as if they'd just slept a night through, could feel the earthquake.

"What?" she said.

He caught enough breath to say, "Cured."

"What?"

"I feel cured."

"Of what? How?"

But he couldn't tell her because it was just shaping itself somewhere behind precise conscious thought, in the place where wounds, real or imagined, were safely nursed without being confronted for years, for decades. It was the sudden rain-fuck which had cured him of the memory-rage her laughter had interrupted. He was grateful.

"I'll tell you later," he said wiping some of the wet from her cheek.

And unspoken but central was his hope that maybe he could feel cured of his flight, retreat; could see himself regaining some courage; get back to the world; away from Prezio whose wounds were scratched into his shoulders; away from this *bruta* place, *bruta* life.

They walked to the car, shoes squishing, hair matted, holding hands but not looking at each other, sheepish, like teen-agers caught in a prank for which they could be punished.

In front of the house their cars were now rain-whipped clean. Outside, on the back patio, the rain had washed away everything but the fragrance of some nameless sweet flower. Maggie asked him what the flowers were, but the flowers were as anonymous to Singer as the birds; a sidewalk New Yorker to the end.

He made a couple of martinis for them which they sipped, watching an astounding yellow and red sunset and swatting away the ubiquitous flies.

Then came a kind of unexpected confessional: Singer reminiscing about his crazy marriage to Christina—all the lies and lovers, Singer and Max playing mother and father to Jessica in Christina's absence and, at the last, her vanishing act; about Jessica's infancy and childhood, a bright child needing private schools they could never quite afford, about her playing with drugs, nothing big but troubling enough.

" 'Memoirs of a *cornuto*' they would call this conversation in Italy," he said making the horn signs on his head. But it wasn't conversation, it was a theatrical monologue, all autobiographical spaces filled in except for the holes left by any mention of Max Messenger, with a silent, attentive Maggie as audience.

He talked about his life in New York, fortunate these days in a rent-controlled loft, now sublet; complained and apologized for the grimy, grungy life in Prezio. Not a mention of the extraordinary events of the day; it was a mutually agreed-upon truce. What Singer did not allow nor Maggie offer were any answers to the questions of the day.

They had not even changed out of their wet clothing. "I'll make the martinis especially dry," he said. He could keep joking now as if one wild orgasmic encounter on grass and gravel and blessed by rain had drained him of remembered rage, of humorless resentment, of unfocused fantasies of revenge. Finally the sun hid beyond the scraggly hills and Maggie shivered. "I'll make us a bite of dinner." It turned out she was a superb cook, turning leftover chicken, eggs and some porcini mushrooms she found in the fridge into a tasty omelet to which feast Singer added the last bottle of Barolo Maggie had bought a few days before; he drank little, she finished most of the bottle. If the martinis had been a monologue, the dinner was a mimeplay. It seemed that if he or Maggie said anything at all it would open floodgates neither of them was prepared for. They ate dinner like an old married couple with a painful history behind them; careful, cool.

At the top of the stairs, again without a word or sign, she followed him into his bedroom. This time the sex, the love, call it what you will, was paced, first tentative, then passionate. In the middle he surprised himself by murmuring, "Are you Max's widow?"

She kissed him and said, against his open lips, "Yes." Then, a second later, "No, no . . ."

They fell asleep immediately after, holding each other like

orphans of a storm neither of them understood. The bed was finally not so enormous.

In the middle of the night he wakes, sensing something unusual. Maggie is leaning on one elbow, awake, staring at him.

She speaks, ice-cold. "What was all that about revenge, you and your friend Mario?"

Singer struggles up from sleep, feels menace in the air, is awake immediately.

"Not Mario. Me. He was just responding to my crazy conversation, my crazy babblings about revenge. Kafka was only a cover."

"Revenge against who?"

"I'm not sure."

"Max?"

"Maybe."

Now she is suddenly as white hot as he'd been in the car when she'd laughed and when the rain began.

"For what? For succeeding when you didn't? For staying on the edge while you played it safe? For becoming so famous after he died?" Her voice is shrill for the first time; she is like a woman in a Greek play, wailing half grief, half unappeasable anger. There are little pools of saliva collecting in the corners of her mouth. Her eyes are almost closed as if she couldn't sustain this level of intimate contempt if she had to make eye contact with Singer. She is naked, both of them having fallen asleep that way, her small cups of breasts absurdly reminding Singer of how he'd held them only a few hours before.

Singer rolls out of his side of the bed and flees to the bathroom to get away from Maggie before saying the next thing he has to say. And there is no doubt that it is something he has to say.

He splashes cold water on his eyes and mouth—at this time of night the faucets only run cold. Next to the bed, Maggie is standing as still as a nude statue. She is calmer now, waiting. "My clothes are in the bedroom downstairs," she says, as if he has demanded an explanation of her nudity.

Now it is Singer who stands in front of her, naked. He says what he has to.

"I know he slept with everyone he could get his hands on." A pause as if there could be some ambiguity, and adds, "He slept with my daughter, with Jessica—Max did."

"My God, oh."

Downstairs Singer took one of Maggie's robes from the guest room and made a middle-of-the-night tea. They have swapped robes; now they can swap Idylls of the King. Maggie seemed to be shaken out of her sudden anger, out of anything but shock and a kind of instant mourning. Singer could see her turning it over and over in her mind: Max and Jessica. It was not to be thought of. It fouled everything.

"At first, when I found out, I was a little out of my mind. It was like knowing that your brother had slept with your daughter. That's why now she's away at boarding school in Florence."

"And that's why you're here? In Prezio?"

"I'm here because my dealer—my former dealer—found a sort of job for me. But I took it because Jessica is at the American School in Florence and I thought maybe I'd get to see her. Oh, Christ, it's hard to unravel. She won't speak to me because I persuaded Max to end it. Give me a break—she was eighteen and he was thirty-seven and substitute father and mother. Maybe I should have butted out, not played the heavy father. God knows what would have happened with them, but at least I'd still have Jessica."

Singer expected some reaction from Maggie, but she just stared at him. He filled her silence with the rest of the midnight story.

"Max actually thought he was in love with her; no one-night

stand or quick affair—he wanted to leave his wife and marry Jessica. I got my ex-wife to chip in and send Jessica to Europe. 'How awfully Henry James of you, Simon.' That's what she said. Christina hadn't been heard from in years—since I got custody—but she could always come up with British aristocratic sarcasm. She also came up with some money for the school—who knows where she got it, she'd been poor for years. 'Not poor, darling, never poor,' she used to say. 'Just broke.'

"Anyway, I sent Jessica away to the American School in Florence. She's been in school for one semester, hasn't written or called. I think she was a little scared, over her head. She was a younger eighteen than a lot of girls. And he'd been her tutor, her cicerone, her Uncle Max all those years; every role in the world except— Then all of a sudden he was something else; it was passionate but it was damned confusing.

"Finally, when the smoke cleared, I didn't really blame Max. For the first and last time that I knew of, he wasn't just getting laid. He fell in love with Jessica. He didn't know what to do, how to handle it. I think he was glad to let me take charge."

She threw back the last of her tea as if it were wine or gin. "Those two," she said. "It must have been hell for everybody." Then—"It's stifling in here."

The windows were all shut against the flies, and for some Prezio-style reason, economy no doubt, there were no screens. Maggie moved to the door, and taking the two of them outside, was probably getting ready to ask tougher questions or make tougher revelations; or perhaps just to get away from such midnight matters. The flagstones were cool and the breeze that came from the hills, blue and scrubby—you couldn't call them mountains—was flower-fragrant. It made Singer realize how they'd both been sweating, her face was sheened over with moisture and his robe (her robe) was sticking to his skin. The moonlight was much brighter than the dim kitchen bulbs.

It showed him a pretty woman's face, a bit older by a year or two than he'd thought; she was maybe early thirties, maybe a touch more.

Singer pulled the damp robe more tightly against the sudden chill. It was, of course, a woman's robe, cotton or some delicate weave. It made him feel what it might be like to be a woman, to wear such slight robes, instead of the big, white, locker-room terrycloth he'd traded for hers. It made him feel that she might be vulnerable, more troubled than her aggressive Max-search made her appear.

"Are you still sticking to the deadline?"

For a minute Singer had no idea what she was talking about. So much had happened since that afternoon, wanting it over, sick of being grilled, unsure whose life was being explored and memorialized; realizing he was being forced to play second banana yet again, issuing a two-day ultimatum. One of those days was now gone.

"So what the hell did you come here for," Singer said, "with your buddy-buddy fake routine about Jessica, with your book and your 'you-don't-know-who-I-am-but-we-have-Max-in-common.' "

"It was true," she said. "It *is* true."

"And Jessica?"

She took a breath between justifications.

"Almost true," she said.

"How can something be almost true?"

"You're the artist. You know about ambiguity and near-truths."

"For example," Singer said.

"I didn't really know her. I tracked her down, went to her school in Florence and took an art class. It wasn't so hard to get in on a day-visit basis. I had a few entry-level bona fides; Max had encouraged me to draw, though he nixed the idea of lessons. I had no idea that she'd— Like a few women, I was in and out of Max's life a lot. I guess Jessica came and went during one of those spaces, times."

"And you became her buddy."

"Well, a school chum anyway."

"All to get to me."

"All to get to you."

"And she told you where I was?"

"Well, no one in New York had any idea where you might be. Not even your dealer."

Maggie sounded aggrieved as if he'd been purposely giving her the slip. "It was as if you'd dropped off the face of the earth."

Now it was Singer's turn to be exasperated. "Didn't you get it? *That was the idea.*"

She sat down and stared at him. She seemed not to know how to respond; took, instead, a swerve. She swung an arm to indicate, not the moonlit hills and sky, but back towards the house.

"That was the idea?" she said. "To sneak away to Pre—whatever this place is called . . ."

"Prezio."

"This grimy house in a rocky moonscape, this grimy house, flies and all. This is where you decide to bury yourself."

"I told you—this is where a job was."

"Some job."

"It pays the rent—sort of."

"Why didn't you sell the painting Max gave you?"

She stepped closer to him, honing in, apparently, on something important to her. "There's a Swiss banker, Roerich, who's paying big bucks for any Messengers. He's in Zurich."

"I heard about Roerich," Singer said. "Did Jessica know you were coming here?"

"I told her I was. Tomorrow's my official departure day, right? How about letting me see the painting!" It was no question, more of an attempt at command. Singer thought, why not let her see it? To her it might be some kind of sacred object. To Singer it was only a missed opportunity; a lost chance for reconciliation.

They were about go upstairs, but not to bed; they would probably go to the cache where Singer kept the painting, though he hadn't entirely made up his mind to show it to her. If he did, he felt, somehow, that the balance would shift, probably in her favor. Singer was not unworldly, not naïve. He had a general notion of how much the piece might be worth. Even before Max died the roll was on. And afterwards, well, death builds and destroys reputations, lowers and inflates prices. Death is the greatest art dealer of all. It was not Singer's line; it had come from Max in the hospital during the second of the two visits Singer had made. Under the pressure of increasing illness Max had given up the irony that had served him so well. His humor had grown as thin as his newly oval face. Now, with a shame-faced grin, he reached back to their earliest time together, kids drunk on the easy romanticism of Thomas Wolfe, of *Look Homeward, Angel, Of Time and the River, The Web and the Rock.*

"Remember," he said with a new quietness in his voice; Max had always spoken a basso profundo; not anymore: "Remember that painting I did when we were still in school—half figurative, half abstract: Elegy For Thomas Wolfe. And remember me, still full of piss and vinegar, full of adolescent borrowed sadness, quoting—I think it was at Don's loft in the Village—" (He lowered his voice in imitation of the moment, soft, ghostly.) " '*Something has spoken to me in the night burning the tapers of the waning year; something has spoken to me in the night telling me that I shall die, I know now where; to find a land more calm than earth, more large than home, towards which the winds are rising and the rivers flow.* ' " Max paused, out of breath? ashamed of his childhood passions? taken by the moment? He sent out a short burst of a laugh, a giggle. "God how solemn we all were. Thomas Wolfe!" Almost the old Max, he went on, "But that was before Death threatened to become my art dealer."

Singer could not remember Max ever having used the word "death" before. Of course a long silence had separated them. In the interim three of their former classmates had "graduated": Joey from a heart attack while rehearsing with his quartet, Don from lymphoma which had forced him to cancel his first one-man show, and Bernice in childbirth, putting a stop to her astonishing success as a painter of portraits of the rich and near-rich. Max and Singer had reminisced, in that reunion way, about their group, their New York gallery and concert and bookstore prowling group, everything before them, big hopes for big names, for big reputations.

"Well," Singer had said, "with some luck you made it past them. You've come out on the up side." Which was when Max had given death the benefit of his slightly depressed art-world aphorism. He'd always been a great one for aphorisms. At one time the group used to have an aphorism-of-the-week club. As Singer recalled it, Max's offerings always took the prize for mordancy; tough ones, ugly ones. Nietzsche: *Thou goest to woman? Forget not thy whip.*

But this was a different Max, perhaps chastened by the brouhaha over Jessica, now months in the past. Neither Max nor Singer could mention it, and both men had assumed they would not see each other again. But the imminence of death was not only an art dealer's issue; it also canceled all debts—of pride, honor, shame. Singer made two visits. The second one was so clearly to be the last that the only feelings Singer had left were a mixed confusion of loss. Rage at betrayal and all such painful abstractions would have to wait. Those were the inner weathers he'd sealed up inside and taken with him on his Italian retreat, the weathers which Maggie had stirred up and turned into an unexpected storm.

Singer paused on the stair. He glanced out of the window, which guarded the foot of the staircase, and saw two startling sights. One was Maggie's car, unused since her arrival, leaning like a cripple on three wheels, the fourth almost entirely flat. The other: in the few minutes since they'd come back into the house the storms had begun again; a black sheet of wind-blown rain swept the road outside.

"Look."

"God almighty—my car!"

"And I've never changed a tire in my life. You don't change tires in New York. There probably isn't a tow place in a hundred miles. Let's wait till the morning and see if the rain lets up."

She turned on him, suddenly ferocious. "If I'm being tossed out tomorrow I want to be ready to go. I'll change the fucking tire."

Huddled in slickers tossed on over their robes, they went out into the rain and Maggie showed him how to change a tire.

"Sudden storms are not uncommon in Umbria at this time of the year—" he began and then shut up.

Feeling foolish, useless, Singer held a flashlight while she jacked up the car. All the while the rain slammed hard against them, rattling against the crippled car. In the weird white light of the flashlight Maggie looked frenzied. This was about more than a tire and a get-away to rescue some self-respect after being told to leave.

"What do you think?" she said. "You think you have a patent on rage against Max? You think you own revenge?" She was out of breath from bending over and pumping. She straightened up and wiped her face of rain and it was soaked the instant after. It was hard to see her expression. She didn't look enraged though, or sound it; it was more like grief than anger. "I'm not Max's widow. My name is not Messenger."

"I see . . ."

"No you don't. I was *supposed* to be Max's widow—wife—widow."

"How can you be supposed to be . . . ?"

"Right, take it in order. I was *supposed* to be his wife. I'd been his graduate student—I think I told you that . . ."

"No, you didn't."

Singer didn't tell her how confused and complicated all her stories were—about herself, about Jessica, certainly about Max. It was hopeless to try and make sense of anything in this mad rain-scene-in-the-dark. She was grunting over the tire, prying off the hubcap. "Engaged—I guess it sounds silly to use that word for Max and anybody, but we were what passed for engaged."

"A ring?" Singer knew he sounded nasty but it wasn't what he felt.

"No ring. By then he was too sick to go shopping even if he'd wanted to. But we had a date set . . . Could you bring that flashlight closer?"

"So you were Max's student?"

"Graduate student, if you please. What's funny?"

"Just that when I took the college route, Max did the laughing. And then he becomes shepherd to a flock of PhDs."

"I wasn't just part of the flock. We were lovers. That old story. The professor and the favorite graduate student."

"But I gather there were others."

"Other favorite students or other lovers?"

"Either."

"There were both. Especially Meredith."

"Ah, at last we get to the Meredith. How much longer will this take? You're soaked."

"So are you. You may as well hear my tale of woe while I get the tire fixed so I can vanish in the morning and take my sad story with me. Meredith is a talented Max-clone . . ." She was kneeling in the mix of mud and gravel, prying the hubcap off. "But I was his wife even without a ceremony. He loved food and he liked mine. Sometimes small things count. We lived together. I began as an 'on the side' when he was still married to what's-her-name . . ."

"Janice?" Singer said. An ex-wife's name was not the first thing you remembered about Max.

"But we got very domestic. Do you realize that if he and your daughter had gotten married *she'd* be the widow now?" This was not something Singer wanted to imagine; he was glad when the pump started pumping and made an awful racket and Maggie disengaged the equipment, stood up and said, "There."

• • •

136

They showered together, neither wanting to wait until the water ran hot. Singer began to soap her and she said, "Good, warm me up a little. Italian rain isn't as cold as British rain but I'm still freezing. When will this fucking water turn hot?"

Singer had no idea, but he began to work on her as if restoring some Renaissance nude: Raphael, Botticelli, except that Maggie was made less amply; small breasts, a delicate rump curving inward. It was an odd way to be erotic but his erection confirmed it to both of them.

She caught a few short laughs in her breath. "Apparently we have more in common than Max."

"Turn around and I'll do your back."

"He married Meredith in the hospital. He betrayed me; he knew I was broke. I was supposed to get the paintings; at least half as the widow's share, even if Meredith or anybody contested the will."

Her back just below the shoulder blades was scratched: gravel marks, mementos of the day's earlier rain, another unexpected crazy intimacy. "Look what I did. You're wounded." Even though he soaped her gently, she winced.

"I've had worse," Maggie said, mysterious.

She turned around in this shower-ballet, her face tilted up to his, streaming with shower water as wildly as it had with Italian rain. "It seems you're the only one who got a Messenger. Now let me do you."

She began to scrub Singer's back. He had scratch marks, too, which she glided over. "*Bruta*," he said. "This place is altogether *bruta*."

The water had turned from cool to scalding in an instant. Singer adjusted the knobs as best as he could. He said, "Why did you come to *me* with this book and all these lies?"

"Fantasies," she said, "not lies. The book was a desperate shot in the dark. There's no contract and it would have to be for a European publisher; Max's base was Europe . . . which means no money or almost none . . ."

"And me . . . ?"

"I was confused, a little crazed. I thought if there was to be a book, maybe . . . you . . . you might be the key."

"Why not all those sensational sex-keys masquerading as graduate students and disciples?"

"They were going to come later. I was all mixed up. I even thought maybe I could get you to write it with me. You've got a reputation . . ."

"Had . . ."

"Okay, take me out of this steaming waterfall. I'm starting to wrinkle up before my time."

He laughed. "I'm shriveling up too."

Maggie looked down. "Gone but not forgotten."

"That seems to be our theme, yours and mine."

The towels were threadbare, absorbing almost no wetness, so they let the sheets do the rest of the drying; he touched her in a number of sensitive places, but more sex seemed beside the point, just then, to both of them and she rolled over onto him pinning him as if to prevent some imagined escape, to murmur, "Listen, I made up a lot of that stuff I said in the shower," and in another of her twists and turns in the art of confession at which she was so skillful, false or true, she said that Max told her so much and so movingly about his closeness with Singer that she thought of filling the empty space inside her with him; it became an obsession. That was the plain and simple truth. All the rest had been her own wild fantasies at one time or another. But they all boiled down to wanting to be with Singer.

"You wanted me to be a Max clone? To fill *you* up with Max-ness, with *our* closeness so you could get into it, too?"

"I don't know what I wanted. I had a little money, not much, no degree yet—I slowed down on that towards the end . . . then stopped . . ." her voice dropped so that he could hardly hear. "Shit! I have no future, nothing planned . . . I'm just hanging in the air."

He said, "Jesus, how can I ever believe anything you say?"

She rolled off him. "I don't know," she says. "Max said I wasn't finished yet; that I was a work in progress."

Singer said nothing. It was as if he had escaped, wasn't there—and in a way he wasn't. He was filled with plans for movement, on fire with a desire to move on. He was like a man saying to his doctor, "Look, I can walk, I can walk." It didn't matter who the doctor had been, maybe the odd woman beside him, touching in her oddness, in how unfinished she was.

He was being pushed back into life. The first step was to get off his ass and go to Jessica. Just go—arrive, appear, confront; it seemed so clear that he should have done that weeks, months ago. And then go back and take up his life where he had left it—if it was still there.

"How did Jessica sound to you—I mean about topic A and me?"

"Hard to tell. Neutral . . . noncommital. But she didn't know me that well."

He took a long time before saying, "I've waited long enough. I wanted to give her her time. Enough space as the kids say."

"You play the heavy father, then the scared modern parent. Why don't you pick one and stick with it?"

He told her what Jessica had been like as a kid, a shy girl, taller than her schoolmates, not pretty but with a long, long swan's neck. She was always cautious, walking on eggs, a skinny, plain, brilliant only child in this crazy household; Christine, her mother, clearly sorry she'd had a child; a disappointed actress, a weaver of tapestries she couldn't sell, a dabbler in Asian mysticism . . . finally picking up men in bars and staying away for days. And with a father mainly in his studio, it must have meant a lot to a marginal young girl to be treated, suddenly, as a central woman by Max. Maybe there was more to her silence . . . Maybe a lifetime of old scores to be settled.

"I'm dropping this game. I'll go see her whether she wants to see me or not."

Maggie had been listening in a somnolent way, almost half-asleep but now, rising to look at him directly, said, "I'll go with you—then all three of us can settle our grudges against Max." It was impossible to tell if she was joking.

"Not me. Count me out of the revenge rat-race." He found himself grinning for the first time in a while. "Life being what it is, one dreams of hope, of reunions, of cured misunderstandings."

"And how about your flight from life, from art, from failure, from success . . . ?"

"Maybe I'll stop thinking in categories. Maybe we should both stop thinking in categories. Life being what it is, one dreams of change."

She fell back and closed her eyes, sinking towards sleep. She murmured, "Don't throw me away. I'm so weary of being up in the air all the time. Please keep me. I'm useful . . . I can change tires . . . I can make omelets out of leftovers . . ." She rolled towards him and a kiss, said, "I'd like to—do it again—but—" and was asleep before she could finish the sentence, exhausted from changing tires, from changing truths.

It was all right. There would be plenty of time for that, after he found his daughter, after he found his courage, lost on the plane to Italy. You didn't throw people away, though he'd been feeling "thrown away" for a long time. He certainly wasn't going to throw away this strangest of surprise gifts breathing heavily beside him— breathing in exhausted bursts as though she'd run a race. He didn't want to think about what being with her might do; tie him, forever, in some incestuous way to Max's shade. She was a work-in-progress. Well, so was Max, even after the end had been written; so was Singer; so was everybody. They might help to complete each other.

Singer, too, was groggy from this craziest of days just ending, almost ready to join Maggie in sleep—perhaps in more than sleep; perhaps in—what?—a future without categories? It stretched before him, a small but uncharted sea in which they both would have to swim until they saw some fresh shore.

This time it was Singer who woke suddenly in the night, remembering that he had never gotten to show Maggie Max's painting; the pilgrimage had been interrupted by the comic drama of a woman changing a flat tire in the wild rain while the Big Strong Man looked on. He'd not looked at the painting himself for a long time. He had no idea why he had to go and look at it just then but he did. It was hidden in the back room on the same floor, not even hung but swathed in bubble wrap and cellophane. Unwrapped, it gleamed at him in the too-bright fluorescent light. Singer had forgotten how compressed it was, how intense the colors, though fading out at the top and towards the bottom into a mix of almost pastel tones, leading to the inscription, *"To my friend Simon Singer with all my love and admiration"*; as if it had been planned all along as part of the composition. It seemed to Singer that relieved of its heavy burden of resentment and reconciliation it was utterly beautiful in its simplicity of means.

A few times in the last year, in his misery, Singer had entertained a desperate, hopeless impulse, almost as disgusting as the idea of throwing someone away. He'd actually thought of destroying the painting. Start clean: tabula rasa. His past with Max was as complicated as any intimate relationship could be; filled with as many mistakes, loyalties, wrong turns, betrayals and lack of forgiveness as any male-female roadway of passion. It was the great American secret: that men could be inside each other's skins without touching those skins; that souls could be joined in holy something-or-other without being married, homosexual or just locker-room buddies; that there was a whole unexplored terrain between men which was its own life, not a parody of the life between men and women: loyalty, pain, secret-sharing, uncompetitive ambition, competitive ambition, mutual pride, betrayal—call it love at the peril of violating the great American ethos of holding hands or touching souls reserved for the Noah's Ark model of women and men.

Singer stood, still naked in the chilly Umbrian night, gazing at the painting for a long moment: destroy? Insane. Even selling it to this Roerich in Zurich to finance, to smooth the journey back to real life, though more reasonable, even that felt ugly. He rewrapped it carefully and put it back in the closet where it was safe from the destructive light, folding it carefully in its protective covering. Let it accompany them, survive them, intact, undestroyed, unsold, an emblem of regret—a hand held towards the future, a silent reminder of how unchangeable the past was, that painful compound of confusion, luck and error against which there are no weapons of any use, least of all revenge.

Back to the bed, no longer so imperially large, just the right size, he slipped in next to Maggie, who murmured something indecipherable and turned towards him as he slipped at last into a rest of his own.

The Exchange

It was the summer of the sweating streets, the summer of the silent computer, of the broken sentences, of the anxious sense of a permanent silence impending. At least that was Mizener's summer. And into this summer she had come, to organize, to help, to distract, to save—Mizener hoped for all of these. After she had organized some of Mizener's traditional chaos, lost drafts, misfiled letters and contracts—after he could find a paper path leading from the confused past to the anxious present, after all this, it turned out she had an urgent request of her own.

He held her off with vagueness and postponements for a week, but she was on her way out of his life and needed an answer. The Saturday before her last week she nailed him.

"So, what do you think?"

"I don't know," Mizener said. "It's a strange idea."

"Not really," she said. "A lot of people in Seattle and Port Townsend are doing this."

"Are they?"

"Mentors are a big thing in the Pacific Northwest."

Tamar had come to Mizener from Port Arthur, through a series of exotic maneuvers—poor Jack Lash's wife had known her ex-husband, and her sudden need for a three-month job meshed exactly with his need for an assistant. She was a touch exotic, herself. For example, leotards though she had to be at least thirty. Purple, tan, and gold leotards, eyes that slanted for no apparent reason, a cupid's mouth sucking ceaselessly on a bottle of Gatorade. She used to play the lute—she proudly showed him the lute-callous on her index finger. And there was her name: Tamar, chosen, she told him carefully, from a poem. It was not clear if it was parent-chosen or self-chosen. Or if she knew that Tamar had lived in the Bible before arriving in a poem.

She finished labeling a file and slid it into the drawer. The file drawer hissed shut.

"Okay," she said. "That's your current stories file. You're up to date."

"Thanks." He was stalling.

"So what do you think?" She closed the space between them and stood shifting her weight, not all that much of it. Mizener, who was always careful to tell the reader details like his characters' height and weight, would have guessed maybe a hundred and twenty pounds. She reached up on tiptoe to replace a book on the shelf next to Mizener's face; a mix of sweat and perfume arrived in the hot, humid air.

"Look, I don't want to push you," Tamar said. "But I've saved some money from these secretarial gigs—and my fiction writing is important to me. I must have spent two thousand dollars on workshops this year. I'm workshopped up to here. I'd rather spend my money this way—and I think you'd be a terrific mentor."

"It's the idea of being paid to be a mentor . . ."

"It would be a favor to me, actually." She was relentless.

"Well," Mizener said. "That's sort of my problem. Money attached to favors—you see what I mean."

She shut her eyes suddenly. He'd noticed that when doing frustrating tasks, shuffling recalcitrant files which refused to yield to her systems, she would often close her eyes in exasperation. When she opened them, something had changed.

"I was afraid you might be a little moralistic about this."

"That's not—"

"I am the world's leading authority on the writing of Maurice Mizener—and you take an almost sensual pleasure in moral positions. God this place is small."

He said, "Tamar, it's been the same size for three months. I can't afford a bigger place. My fiction is too moral."

"Now you're angry."

"No, but I'm damned hot. How about we have some air conditioning?"

"I hate that sterile freezing. You promised."

"When I promised it wasn't ninety degrees."

"The paper says eighty."

It was an argument born the day she arrived clutching what turned out to be the ubiquitous bottle of Gatorade. Energy, she'd explained, unasked. She'd brought vitamins, an insistence on all natural foods, leotards in many colors, and the energy needed to straighten his papers out, no small task. She'd also brought a Pacific Northwest hatred of air conditioning.

Unnatural, she'd said. Fresh air is fine, hot or cold. Comfortable, he'd replied. Neither natural nor unnatural. Just comfortable.

She'd won because of his need. He had persuaded himself that if he could ever get his papers straightened out he would be able to climb out of the hole he was in; would be able to understand what writing prose was, again, galvanize the book of stories, finish the novel whose advance was long since spent, get his thoughts in a straight line again, find a lyric or comic conclusion, best of all both at once. It had been a terrible time, all right. Never, never had he had such a spell, such a time in which the actual idea of writing down the simplest of sentences seemed so hopeless, foolish, without meaning, the only continuous meaning he'd ever counted on, gone as suddenly as the heat lightning of that terrible summer.

He had written to Marie Lash, Jack's widow—who'd finally sent him Tamar. It was coming to that, his friends having widows and him in his forties for God's sake: a thought connected in Mizener's mind to his writing dying on him. "I don't know what Jack would have said, writing coming so naturally to him, everything came so naturally to him, but I can't get myself to believe it matters that I spend the time of my life on earth writing down 'She opened the door' or 'summer afternoon.' If you can't write something like 'she opened the door' or 'summer afternoon,' the world is a bleak place and you can't do anything and you certainly can't end up with 'It was the best of times, it was the worst of times' or 'For a long time I used to go to bed early.'" It was the most painful letter he'd ever written.

Marie had suggested that Tamar, Jack's student and secretary, bringer of order, might be the answer. And when the answer to your troubled life insists on no air conditioning—you sweat.

"You are angry," she repeated.

"No, bewildered. Let's look for help in my favorite place."

He pulled down a fat book. She smiled.

"The Bible?"

"The dictionary."

Mizener rustled the pages of his old friend.

"Here—Mentor. Experienced and trusted advisor."

"Ha." Tamar apparently felt vindicated. "Presidents have experienced and trusted advisors. And they get paid."

"Look, I can always use some typing. Can you handle the Mac?"

She shook her head. Her eyes were closed again, but this time they were closed shut the way children shut their eyes—the end of the world. Mizener unbuttoned the top button of his shirt and flapped his arms gently to dissipate the gathering sweat.

"There has to be a way," Tamar said. "You could see yourself as a mentor to me, couldn't you? It's just a question of doing it for money, right?"

He sat on the couch, a place he never used; he needed a neutral zone. It smelled musty, like a reproach.

"Sure—I haven't lost everything I know about how to do it. I just can't seem to do it, myself, these days."

"I know. It's temporary. All men have this problem, sometimes. It goes away. You get it back."

"All men," Mizener said, wondering what he had going here.

"All of the writers I've worked with have been men. A coincidence, I guess."

Tamar sat down on the couch, too sweatily close to him. Feeling like a dumb, lecturing mentor, he said, "Listen, there's a kind of natural space between people . . ."

"It's different in different countries," she said.

Anxious, he made a joke out of her inappropriate closeness. "You expect this from Mediterranean people. Not from Port Townsend."

"Oh, for God's sake . . ."

He swerved in self-defense. "Did you know Jack Lash very well?"

A jagged slash of heat lightning split the sky outside the window.

"Well enough. I liked him and he liked me. He was a restless soul."

The answer satisfied Mizener although he doubted it would satisfy Marie Lash.

"Jack was sort of fed up with Port Townsend. If he hadn't had that heart attack something else would have taken him away from there."

"Did you . . . ?"

"Listen," she said. "This is important enough for me to think in different categories."

He listened for more thunder. "Wasn't that somebody's last words? Some great writer," Mizener said. "Think in different categories?"

"I don't know. You're the mentor," Tamar said.

"Not yet."

"Then suppose I pay in ways you might need—but wouldn't involve money?" Her legs were curled under her arms, fetal-natural. A caress of sweaty calf touched Mizener's hand. "Would you be my mentor, then?"

"What makes you think I need that? I mean any more than anybody else?"

"I didn't say you needed it any more than anybody else."

He felt he might be blushing and felt foolish at the idea, but there was no way to test it. "Listen, Tamar," he said. "I'll give you all my wisdom in one sentence. Read every book you can get your hands on. Keep a notebook and take notes on every experience, even better, everything you imagine, that can help you into fiction and when you've written a draft keep revising till you can't do it any more, then stop. There! Now you know what I know. You don't need a mentor."

"I never saw you use a notebook."

"That's because I'm stuck."

"You mean blocked."

He shivered, staring out the window at the sky.

"Don't use that word. I usually use a notebook. When I'm alive."

"Maybe I can bring you alive."

"I thought I was too moral."

"That's up to you, isn't it?"

She stood suddenly and put some distance between them.

"You must think I'm crazy to put so much pressure on for this."

"No, but I do wonder—"

"I'm stuck in the same way. Oh, it's not the same, I suppose. I'm on the bottom rung of the ladder. I'm not even on the ladder, yet. But I was going great for a while. Jack was reading my stuff and guiding me. Then, it—just stopped on me. Not a word."

"Maybe you've got the answer yourself—you just have to keep trying, and wait for the return button."

She turned a steady stare of large gray-green eyes on him. "Suppose I, or suppose anybody, said the same thing to you?"

Mizener shrugged. "It's different. We're in different places, different times."

Tamar came back to the couch. Mizener stood up. His trousers were sticky with sweat between his legs when he moved. He was thinking of ways to change the flow of talk; another direction, any direction, even silence. But she was ahead of him, as she had been from the start.

She stood in front of him, head turned up towards his eyes. "How close," she said, "is too close in the USA?"

It turned out that leotards came off with less difficulty than he'd thought. It turned out that Mizener could forget the astonishing heat in the heat of touching Tamar and being touched by her. And afterwards he wondered if he had been touched enough to make a story, an anecdote, a sketch, something of the surprising experience, something which might surprise him back into the flow of words. Any motif might do to jump-start his writing head: feeling guilty about the difference in their ages, the coincidence of Tamar and he having the same trouble at the same time, the fact of his now having signed on, willy-nilly, as her mentor—he ran his fingers over the ripples of thoughts but nothing stayed the way the memory of the callous on her finger, her lute-callous, lingered. Only that, he thought, imagine! The roughened, sandpapery touch of a callous. And instantly the old despair returned.

Tamar kissed him and vanished into the bathroom. Mizener waited, nervously, as if there was something to continue. The heat, forgotten in the heat of the moment, returned with an oppressive wet weight. Now that it was over, now that he knew she'd been wrong, that there was no payout for him other than the moment's pleasure and only an obligation left, he was impatient.

Five minutes passed, maybe more. Impatience grew into anxiety. He needed for her to come out of the bathroom, he didn't quite know why. It was as if each added moment of her prolonged absence underlined his failure to transform a surprising, slightly grubby incident into something to feed his starved imagination; what he saw now as a foolish, momentary fantasy.

Mizener forced himself to wait; he stood up and waited a little more, shifting his weight from side to side. He was, in some ways, a shy man; not the sort to pound on a bathroom door with a young woman inside. He actually listened but heard nothing—just a faint rustling; clothing being adjusted, perhaps toilet tissue. Embarrassment fought with anxiety; anxiety won.

He called her name. No response. "'Tamar, are you okay?" he called out. In the ensuing silence he rapped on the door, finally knocking louder, harder. Could she have horribly regretted the deal, the proposed exchange, could she be doing something awful to herself in a moment of despair? In desperation he pushed at the door and it swung open.

Mizener stood in astonishment, staring at Tamar who sat on the closed commode in a welter of ink-scribbled pages, some in the sink, some on the floor. Some pages had been hurled so far, apparently in a frenzy, that he had to avoid stepping on them as he moved towards her. Once again he spoke her name.

She looked up at him for an instant, a crazed, wild look; the look of someone, an animal perhaps, released from a trap. Her mouth was open, that mouth which had done such sensual improvisation only moments ago, but now hung open in absolute distraction. Then her head was again bent over her frantic writing, lips pursed, eyes squinting in concentration. With or without Mizener present she was alone. Mizener stooped and picked up one of the pages then dropped it without a glance. He wiped a sheen of sweat from his forehead and stood frozen in place, eyes fixed trancelike on the young woman. At last he cried out in despair, "Tamar, Tamar, my God."

Tamar stared at him. She looked surprised that he was still there. "It worked," she called out, as if she were bringing some wonderful news he'd been waiting for. Mizener tasted something sweet and sour on his tongue—the flavor of her kisses mixed with some new knowledge. The taste of irony, he thought, the literary man to the end, needing a trope to make an experience real.

Staying in this vein, he said, "Using a pen, Tamar? Permanent ink?"

She gazed at him, at last registering his presence. "I've been stuck on this story for a year. Thank you, thank you, thank you . . ."

"Any time," Mizener said with a dry smile, but Tamar took no notice.

At the bathroom door, a quick turn back. She was again scribbling as if frantically transcribing some cosmic dictation. He gazed at this young, writing nymph freed by a reluctant, older satyr. Sweat dripped from her eyes; he wondered how she could make out the words on the page. It was unclear if it was sex-sweat or writing-sweat. It didn't matter.

Frozen in the doorway, Mizener said, "I'm glad it was good for you."

She threw him a triumphant smile.

Time Will Tell

The trouble starts on the last day of the trip when Maurice buys
the watch on Market Day at Sarlat. Their exploratory trip on
which so much depends is going exceptionally well, time suspended,
the June days warm, blessed by sun, full of amazement: castles
keeping solemn watch above a restless river, the ancient caves at Lascaux startling with another, a deeper kind of dank suspended time.

Lascaux was closed to the public except for a few hours a day and
even then you needed a special dispensation to get in. Maurice had a
friend in management at Sotheby's who knew an art historian at
Columbia—and here they were.

In the chill dark of the cave Rosa gazes at the slender-legged
hunchbacked shapes of bison moving in mysterious procession across
the stone walls, at an anonymous but unmistakable hand print. She
breathes, "Thirteen thousand years ago. Impossible to imagine. I
can't believe I'm here."

"Terrifying," Maurice says. "Beautiful," as if they were the same
thing.

They'd called the trip exploratory but of course what Maurice
and Rosa are after is some kind of confirmation. That they love each

other is understood—though, naturally, what each of them under-stands by the word is not entirely clear, may never be clear. But now marriage is in the air, a sweet, distant scent, not without a whiff of danger. To bring it closer and to defuse it, they need only, say, a trip to the Dordogne together. The unspoken sexual anxiety that is to be tamed by travel, exciting but complicated by Maurice's self-conscious concern, is not entirely the stuff of bodies, not entirely of the spirit. It is what Rosa's philosophy thesis director calls the Mind-Body problem.

They'd put it down to the recent spate of deaths: the men in his family died young, his father at forty-four, his grandfather never having made it to forty. Most recently it had been the man who'd taught Maurice what he knew about art: his Uncle James, attacked by his heart and struck down at fifty-one. He'd never been able to tell more than the bare facts, who died when—had never unleashed the one telling phrase she was waiting to hear, an attitude, an insight. He was better at jokes and charm. His answer to the dark intruder breathing down his neck seemed to be style.

At his uncle's funeral Rosa could see Maurice, thirty-six years old and counting, sitting, back bowed in self-reflexive curve, Maurice mourning for himself in advance. Rosa was quickly realizing that she'd fallen for a man who in spite of his trigger wit, heard the clock ticking at every moment. She had seen his vast and varied collection of watches—anxiety masquerading as a hobby—much of it gleaned from his work as art auctioneer; free-lance, Sotheby's one week, Christie's the next. More to the point, she had seen him throw off his clothing eager to celebrate the moment of love, naked as a babe except for the watch on his wrist: permanent, unavoidable, like a tattoo.

It seemed to her an emblem of the awkwardnesses, the wrong touches at the wrong moment, the infelicitous turns and finally the too early or too late climaxes. One afternoon, as they were sleepily groping towards each other, falling dizzily into the pit of sensual pleasure, Rosa felt herself almost falling away, the two of them side by side now, felt Maurice falling with her, then, her eyes flickering open, she saw Maurice glancing at his watch. Never, she thought, it will never be the same again. Afterwards she questioned herself, her acuity: had he perhaps been gazing past his wrist, his watch, in sightless, glazed-eyed passion? Was she becoming obsessed more than Maurice? Paranoid? But of course it was the same again, the next time; the wonderful forgetfulness of touch and connection.

After a while she found herself wondering how many times—when her eyes were shut in pleasure—was he actually checking his watch, a secret vice of anxiety, betraying her with time instead of a woman? It was an intolerable burden, this balancing of his love for her and his involvement with time. How much pleasure was he taking from her? How much was he allowing himself to keep? It was all a terrible tangle. Or to put it more directly, in Rosa-style when she was taking a break from philosophical categories—was she involved with a nut? A nut to whom the world was one great, round ticking watch.

She was twenty-nine, a graduate student enmeshed in recovering the now-bypassed school of existentialism; her friends were doing work on Julia Kristeva and Francois Lyotard, hip, feminist, post-everything. But for Rosa musty names like Sartre, Camus, and Merleau-Ponty were alive in her head, on her computer. Her dear, donnish, widowed father, now retired from his job as headmaster of an experimental private school in Shreveport, was dry, irritable in his estimation of her efforts. She'd called him to tell of her thesis choice.

"Be careful, daughter-mine," he'd said. "I've been hoping you'd start showing signs of your grandmother's temperament. Fiery, decisive . . ."

"I know, Dad. I've been hearing about her since I was little. I guess I have my own way, whatever that is."

"I'm just cautioning you, as a teacher and your old man. Be careful you're not just echoing your personal style by choosing your somewhat forgotten beloved French philosophers."

"And what style is that?"

"It can't be news that you have difficulty making decisions, getting off the dime, taking action. You delayed so long getting back to graduate schools with your forms you're lucky Columbia was either absent-minded or tolerant . . ."

"Oh, please . . ."

"You've been known to fast and pray over which appetizer to order so long that the rest of the table is ready for dessert."

"Exaggerations of a slight tendency."

"Hah! How many years have you been working on your thesis? Is the end in sight? Are you going to be nursing babies before you have your degree?"

She was patient. Rosa admired her father for his differences from her—direct where she was circuitous; she trusted him. She said, "So you're saying existentialism is a lot about the freedom of action . . . ?"

"Or lack thereof."

"Then maybe I've picked just the right guys."

But she'd considered herself warned, was worried about why the ending of her thesis kept receding, the closer she got. She had become a close Rosa-watcher, had learned that if you didn't trust yourself, naturally, with ease, you became wary of others. But you could, apparently, be in love and wary at the same time. You'd think she'd know by now—a veteran of several brief affairs and two long ones. Each man had been off-center, obsessive in some way—that was the model of what she now thinks of as "Rosa's man." Someone who becomes very intense over something very small—usually the same thing, over and over again.

By now she knows, too, that everyone has one quirk or another about sex—there were no final standards of measurement—except

perhaps spontaneity, affection, concern; and even those were nego-
tiable in special circumstances. Which leaves a a lot of room for indi-
vidual craziness, the craziness adding spice to the taste, provided the
particular spice was to your taste. Hence, Maurice, time, watches, and
the nut-question.

In search of solutions she was the one who'd suggested a pre-wed-
ding trip. Maurice had never been to France so France was his choice.

"But my French is vaguely Cajun, and the French hate it when I
talk. They think it's like pig-Latin," Rosa had said.

"Good. Mine is from high school. Nonexistent. We'll be thrown
completely on each other. What better test?"

She knew they weren't talking about linguistic skills. Rosa was
from a small town in Louisiana, near Shreveport; an anomaly, an
Italian family in Cajun territory—slow-talking, languorous, she was
often as late as a half hour for appointments. Their first evening
together Rosa observed that Maurice kept glancing at his watch. Was
he bored, or was it because of his job: running art auctions, time
being central to the occasion, or at least an exquisite sense of timing?
Later on Rosa could not credit the notion that his watch-watching
while making love was a sign of boredom. It was not just that her
senses could feel a hard contradiction to that idea; it was also her general sense of their affection, their responses.

Still, this network of subtle spyings, of shared anxieties, of tense
time-hauntings had blossomed into a kind of sickness—infecting the
bedroom most of all. The trip to France might be the cure.

Which is why the incident at the Sunday Marché at Sarlat is so
troubling to Rosa. In the middle of a feast of plenty—baskets filled
with scarves of Provençal design, spicy sausages, collarless shirts—a
universe of exotic goodies, Maurice heads right for a long table set
out with a universe of watches.

"Look." He holds up a watch with an enormous dial. "What do
you think?"

Rosa pauses; she holds up a shawl covered with fleur-de-lys, then allows her glance to drift towards Maurice. "Well," she says, "you can tell the time from across Fifth Avenue with that one, if that's what you have in mind."

He buys it anyway; no haggling. It is on his wrist in minutes, large, aggressive, a statement as much as an instrument: Time rules.

The argument doesn't happen until hours later, when they are hunched over menus and the *International Herald Tribune* at a gentle little brasserie in the tiny Centre Ville, near a wetly whispering fountain.

"I thought," she says in a very quiet voice, "that we were going to turn off, turn away from all that."

"All that?" Maurice says, utter innocence, distracted by the decision between an omelet with a foie gras pâté or a simple sandwich jambon and a Coke.

"You know this place can actually give you too much foie gras, not to mention walnuts."

"Please, Maury, no games. Not only another watch—but an enormous dial. What's going on?"

"Do you want me to sing 'as time goes by'? We have to take each other as we are, in small things, anyway."

Rosa takes a deep breath. "Remember," Maurice says, refusing to relinquish his smile under pressure, "the guide book says that the Thirty-Years War started here. We have to be very careful."

He maneuvers her back into the Utah question. "Listen," he says, "Suppose Utah happens. What do we do?" Utah is his half-assed symbol for what might happen if and when she gets her doctorate, gets a job offer and it's in some benighted place where there are no auction houses. Who goes where?

She goes along with his swerve, is very careful, saving her firepower for the evening, unwilling to spoil the day. The afternoon swims by in a suspended haze. In a canoe on the river they float by small sandstone villages, the shadows of tall poplars click past them with metronomic regularity. Worn out by their inability to decide which oar will propel and which will steer, they drift happily in the vague bee-buzz, sun-and-shade-patched afternoon, below the indifferent chateaux perched on passing slopes.

She murmurs, "All this prehistory . . ."

"Yes," Maurice says. "If time started here it seems to stop here, too . . ."

Rosa lets the remark rest quietly in the air between them. The afternoon sun has drained all confrontation from her even though she sees the electric glint of sunlight on the silver circle of the giant timepiece on his wrist, where his hand, large, claiming, lies on her knee.

Later, still pleasantly lazy, they decide to have dinner at the hotel, which sits next to a small echo of the great rush of river they'd been on all afternoon. Dinner is served along the riverbank and Rosa's generosity in extending Maurice the loan of a few hours after their argument is repaid. Over espresso he is the absolute charmer she'd first met on line at the multiplex on Third Avenue—happily horrified at allowing herself to be picked up. He'd done some routine or other, she's long since forgotten what, except that it made her laugh and now, tonight, he does a new one: he plays the art auctioneer, but this time he is auctioning the absurdly pink and yellow sunset, the enchanting sound of the river, an orphan tributary of the Dordogne along which their hotel had been built and by whose banks they had eaten the inevitable foie gras—this time served warm, scattered with grapes and breathing cognac, including the inevitable walnuts and accompanied by a second bottle of the joyful Bordeaux.

"How much, how much I ask you for this astounding, sweet bird-song? How much for the last touches of French sunlight on this unassuming but absolutely handsome river?" He is out of his chair now circling the table towards her, tall, eccentric, hair uncombed as usual. None of the of the other hotel guests look up to notice, except for the rotund Patronne on her high stool at the juncture of the hotel and the outdoor dining area; she shrugs—perhaps as accustomed to oddball men as Rosa.

"And how much for the smile of this lovely young woman, the rough music of whose voice can make the heart stop?"

Rosa is trying not to laugh, trying to nurse the return of her noontime anger, her dismay, but she's drunk more wine than she can easily handle and the cheese has not even arrived yet, and she lets his charm past her guard even though his mock auctioneer's arm carries the morning's watch, a moonlike reminder of the trouble they're in.

He leans over her. "One million dollars is a modest evaluation, ladies and gentlemen. I will ask who bids one million dollars. Ah, the lady in the white pants and blue sweater with the million dollar smile. One million once, one million twice . . ."

He bends down for his kiss-as-reward. "One million dollars three times. Done!"

She reminds herself, as she has so often in recent months, that Maurice is walking a tightrope on the edge of an abyss, the men in his family vanishing all around him. And she kisses him back feeling foolish and hopeful at the same time.

The wine makes their bed quickly for them that night. Stumbling around in the darkened room, large, with the strangeness of French country inns, musty and faintly lavender-smelling all at once, round little tables in the wrong place, the bedstead on a wooden platform so they bump their knees as they circle each other, woozily removing first a piece of each other's clothing, then one of their own. Finally, they find the one familiar place, four arms and legs make a nest in the sagging center of the enormous ancient bed. Lips and hands losing and finding their way in the dark—why hadn't they thought of wine before, Rosa wonders, New York Puritans of the middle-class, always searching out serious solutions to serious problems. Why not mix and match—a frivolous solution to an intense worry? They play with peripheries for a while, sensitive skin at earlobes, behind knees, the forgiving charm of the earlier evening fueling an easy desire. In a few moments peripheries give way to more central urgencies, the opening, accepting, joining, the oscillation between giving and taking back—in remembering this night, later, Rosa will allow only such euphemisms to evoke the moment—all suddenly interrupted by the gliding of Rosa's hand across Maurice's arm as he reaches down to touch her, sliding the rough reminder of the new watch on his wrist across her flesh.

Wordless, she tries to grasp the clasp of the watchband, to remove this intrusive witness to something absolutely private. The clasp does not give, Maurice pulls back. "What?" he murmurs, rising from a distant, watery place.

"No," she says meaning "off." He doesn't understand, struggles to keep the watch where it is, accidentally scratching the back of her hand and desire collapses like a child's pyramid of playing cards, the promise of building it again always a promise of future pleasure. But not tonight!

While he rummages through his travel kit for a band-aid he tells her about his father's death, still young, losing heart, heartweary— literary expressions from books tell it better than medical terms, he says. Then he allows himself the closest thing to a try at under- standing. "My father's heart failed him, like his father's had and his brothers. He left me his watch and I found myself adding to it— buying watches and performing a magic safety ritual at the same time."

"But why all the time—even in bed?"

Maurice shrugs. "You're the philosopher. I don't know. An extra pulse, maybe? In case the regular one fails. Maybe I'm mixed up about organs, heart, prick, damned if I know . . ." He wrestles her back into the chaos of messed-up sheets and blankets. "Listen," he says. "As I once told Socrates, the overexamined life is not worth living. I exercise, my cholesterol is championship level, I have checkups, I'm in great shape, I don't even get colds. But maybe you don't want to stay in this with a guy whose ticker may be ticking faster than other men."

"I've seen other men," Rosa says. "Don't try to sell me other men."

"Good," he says. "It's a harmless lunacy. Don't let it kill anything."

Rosa is now sympathetic, her frustration has melted into a desire to understand; only the still throbbing scratch on her wrist keeps her restless, keeps her from falling back into the Laocoon tangle of sheets for another try. By the time Maurice has fallen asleep she is still wide-awake.

She pulls out her never-absent laptop and tries to work on her thesis, the ending, so close but still so far—but she drifts . . . It is, for the moment, impossible to work seriously. Never mind the mind-body problem, here is the love-work problem. For the moment the two have become one and Rosa gives up. She is sure she will not be able to sleep, but she feels herself drifting off—the wine, overconfidence in her lover's charm, his sincerity, or just the habit of hope built against loss, it was hard to say.

A month before the trip Rosa had moved in with Maurice; all kinds of trials and tests had been in the air and they were still working out whose stuff went where—so it was a bit like hotel life. Of course, one of the first things he'd done, once she was ensconced, was to take her through his collection: timepieces from all over the world, including his father's Rolex, winking in its gold circle behind the glass case. There was a watch from Holland with its works all exposed, like a person's chest cavity during an operation; there was a tiny, tiny watch from Switzerland whose face could only inform you of the time if you peered at it through the little magnifying glass fastened to its side by a miniature gold chain; there were watches that buzzed and chimed on the quarter hour, on the half hour. Maurice gave her the guided tour as if they were in the Uffizi gallery in Florence.

No one could say she hadn't been warned.

By the second day they are back the vacation has vanished from their bodies and souls; unpacking, jet-dragged, Maurice was instantly pressed, out of the blue, into a marathon auction for the New York branch of a German art auction house, Rosa dizzy with meetings at Columbia—her thesis director, her own students whose problems have piled up during her absence.

For the first week back neither of them give sex a passing thought. Only once when Rosa, on the way from the bathroom back to the bedroom, after brushing her teeth, passes the glass case where Maurice keeps his prized collection of watches, does she allow herself a quick twinge, a sense of seriously unfinished intimate business.

They'd arrived in New York on a Friday and by the following Friday they collapse together. "We need a vacation," Maurice murmurs, flinging his pants onto a chair—not his usual meticulous self. Rosa is alert, watching him carefully. She has a plan, formed as she observes Maurice taking off the Sarlat watch and placing it on the nightstand.

Wearing only her bra she stands over him as he sits, limply, on the edge of the bed.

"Hey," she says, "I remember you. Aren't you the guy who auctioned off the sunset in Sarlat?" And follows this with a bending-down kiss, full of closed-eyes tongue surprises. Then she unhooks her bra and tosses it on the nightstand, covering the watch. Maurice is beat but he's not dead. He rises to the occasion murmuring mysterious endearments in German. "You don't speak German," she whispers trying not to tear the moment with laughter.

"It's the auction—" He reaches to pull her down. "Klimt, Schwitters, this week the whole world is German."

"Ein minute," she says and vanishes into the bathroom to perform her diaphragm ballet. "A diaphragm," Maurice had snorted, the first time. "You're so retro." But Doctor Ames had banned the pill and they were long past the condom stage of intimacy and trust—still neither of them wanted the interruption of a child before they know what the grown-ups are really up to, before she's finished her thesis, maybe has a job. When she returns, delay has not cooled the moment. Rosa is thrilled: this is illicit, untimed, watchless love; until, in the instant before the lamp is switched off, she sees that while she was squatting, inserting the lubricated rubber circlet, he has retrieved the great circle of time and strapped it back onto his wrist. They are, it seems, truly going around in circles.

Her vision blurs, rage replacing any developing desire. It has also replaced speech. She is reduced to pointing. Maurice doesn't need words by this time. He acknowledges defeat, rolls over and, wiped out by the latest skirmish in the watch-wars, by a week of Klimt and Schwitters, is asleep in three breaths.

Like a sleepwalker Rosa stands in the living room, naked, in front of the glass case in which the enemy rests, unsleeping. Her breath is tight in her chest and she is on the edge of tears but unwilling to weep and lose without a chance of winning. Her shoes are in the bedroom and she dashes back in, retrieves one. She is going to fight back. Her grandmother's temper, the Italian-Irish mixture which had given birth to family legends of wild brawls followed by God knows what kind of reconciliations—the temper she'd thought had skipped several generations—is apparently alive and well and about to spread glass and watchworks over the entire living room floor.

The first attack is noisy but ineffectual. She ransacks the case, grabbing watches, smashing at them with the heel of her shoe. Nothing. Then she remembers the utility drawer in the kitchen, replete with wrenches, Phillips screwdrivers—and a hammer. The first victim is Maurice's father's Rolex. Raising the hammer, Rosa knows she may be saying good-bye to more than an expensive watch, may be shattering every hope and plan born in the past seven months, may be destroying the works that make her life go around these days.

The first blows do nothing but raise a spider's web around the glass casing—or was it plastic? Rosa has no idea, cares less. In her present state she could smash the universe to pieces. By the time she'd taught herself how high to raise the hammer and how to rap the case smartly so that shards of whatever it was sprayed the floor, Maurice stands, staring with bleary eyes, only half awake, at some nightmare of the end of time.

A child of six, he had stood, shocked into stillness, while his mother smashed the locked credenza searching for the last bottle of scotch in the house, in the world; had stood, again, staring, helpless, while his college roommate thrashed on the EMS stretcher in some unexplainable fit. But he would not be helpless now. This is not an end he will take without a fight

"Son of a bitch," he whispers in horror, "what the hell are you doing?"

"I'm saving your fucking life," Rosa says, aware that she is committing a double-entendre, that Maurice's "life" and his "fucking life" are two distinct entities—though both are, perhaps, in need of salvation. She is, even in the heat of battle, the P.I.T.—her classmates' self-mocking acronym—instead of a princess, a philosopher in training.

But Maurice, eyelids sticky with sleep, is able to take in only one entendre. He is a middle-of-the-night phenomenologist—what he sees is the only reality. All he knows is that Rosa, the woman he wants to marry—the only woman he has ever wanted to marry—is smashing his precious watch collection to fragments of glass and plastic.

He grabs her arm, raised, poised for another hammer blow.

"My God, Rosa. What . . . ?"

She accepts the pause and answers, "You know damned well what—"

She breaks free and flails even more wildly, a perverse joy in the sounds of breakage: the clips, the crunches, the pops, her breath coming faster, hotter. Maurice tries to hold her again, this time pulling her to him, the two of them naked, skin slippery, sweaty, strange, her anger not half spent, needing him to be involved in this action somehow. He feels this without interpreting it, grasps her harder, kissing her, almost biting her lip, to taste her rage as much as to stop it; her arm is now limp at her side, still clutching the hammer. They slip, fall to the floor, risking multiple lacerations, not giving a damn, glued together by the wild excitement of attack and counter-attack. They make what you could not exactly call love, but with the same grammar of touch and movement as making love, for once with no anxiety, no self-conscious concern, no distraction: time has, for the moment, been smashed to a stop.

Afterwards, they lie like two characters in some old surrealist film, the floor around them a carnage of crystal shards, numbers, both Roman and Arabic, scraps of ripped cardboard, torn plastic and shattered metal casings.

Rosa lies there, baffled by the achievement of the pleasure and the knowing how little Maurice's obsession matters. The trick, it seemed, was to get beyond, to the other side. Where they could begin.

"You owe me twenty thousand dollars," he says, sleepily beneath a half-yawn. "That's what that collection was worth."

"I'll pay it," she says. "After we're married." A pause. "A dollar a week."

Then, as if suddenly waking up after a violent nightmare she picks a sliver out of her thumb—glass or plastic she is not sure which, and looks around at the battlefield, covered with the corpses of Bulovas, Rolexes, of exotic Swiss names she does not know and cannot pronounce.

"My God," Rosa says, horrified. The hammer lies near her foot, touching it. In disgust she kicks it away and rises on one elbow, looming over Maurice, an apologetic ghost. "Listen," she says. "I can't believe I did that . . . I'm so sorry . . . I know how much those watches meant to you . . . all those years of collecting and caring . . . And all because . . ." She knows she is babbling on but she has no brakes available at the moment. Maurice provides the brakes, turning slowly on his side, looking up at her, and extends his arm beneath Rosa's gaze. He carefully removes the Sarlat watch and hands it to her, an obscure offering at the end of an even more mysterious ritual. She gazes at it as if it were an object from another planet, then lays it gently on the floor next to her. Her rush of words is stilled.

Maurice lies back and closes his eyes as if this has been a great effort. Rosa waits, holds her breath, actually. In the seven months she has known him he has never done anything so simple and open, so unprotected by charm or wit. But there is nothing more to wait for. Maurice is fast asleep, yet again. He was always falling asleep, could do it on a dime, not just after sex, all the time, without needing the usual preambles to drifting off; eyes closed, a fluttering semi-snore troubling his upper lip and he was off—the ultimate overtired New Yorker pressed too hard by work, by being single and the need to arrange an evening as well as a daytime work-life. He would doze off next to her at the movies, sometimes even at the theater at seventy-five dollars a ticket. When a friend asked, early on, "Are you sleeping together," Rosa could only answer, "You don't know the half of it."

As if appointed by some university dean in the sky, she feels in charge now, gets him to his feet, waking him enough to get him off the floor and into the bedroom without tearing the delicate fabric of his sleep, like taking a child from one place to another in the middle of the night. Rosa will remember this moment a dozen years later, carrying her little girl in from the car one winter's night, upstairs into a chilly bed, trying not to wake her as she scrunches blankets all around her in the still cold house, hearing her husband turning the thermostat on, the roar coming up, like a fire catching.

Maurice tumbles into the bed onto his side, his breathing measured again, and Rosa lies awake and does what all philosophy students are supposed to do: she thinks.

Thinks in her mother tongue, irony: The existentialists were right. Only they somehow missed how funny it all was. It's too hard to share this world with others. It's too comically awful that making love has to be done together. What an insult, what a giving over of autonomy. That's what her existentialists were so busy with—your freedom ends where somebody else's skin begins. It's even worse when the skin belongs to someone who has sparked what we call love . . . and how she did love Maurice's skin, his arms and legs dotted with tufts of hair, the slightly swarthy face . . . thick veins on the hands . . . it was even worse when that skin is sporting a time bomb that won't go away, like an enchanted clock in a new kind of fairy tale.

It seems that it doesn't matter about getting somebody else to do something: take off a watch, move towards life instead of death. It just matters what you do! She would not be one of those weird fifties characters in Sartre's novels—frozen in inaction because any act was as meaningless as any other act. The outcome might not be any more than shards of glass and metal and a stunned lover—perhaps even an ex-lover. But it had put a finish to a fake pre-honeymoon.

She had it now—and it might lead her to the elusive ending for her never-ending thesis. Maurice had given her the clue, with all those heart failures behind him and perhaps ahead of him. Maybe the trick was to reverse it. Maybe the trick was for you not to fail your heart. And to do that you had to act. If that was the Classic Comix version of Sartre's Being and Nothingness or Heidegger's Existence and Time, then that's what it would have to be.

Rosa smiles on the edge of sleep. She would like to get out of bed, boot up her computer and jot down these notes towards the ending of her thesis. But by now she is exhausted, fit only to join Maurice in his closing down of consciousness for the night.

In the morning she would call her father and tell him she'd gone from Existentialism to Pragmatism, from Sartre to William James in a few sharp hammer blows. That would get his attention . . .

One last surprise. When she spoons down next to Maurice, he does a half-turn and starts talking. "Hey . . . what will we do," he whispers, ". . . you do your stuff, get your degree and you get a job in Utah or somewhere? No auction houses in . . ."

But he has forgotten that he is not really awake, does not wait for an answer, and anyway, at this moment Utah is the stuff of dreams. Now they are both asleep, safe, for at least one night, free from the awful ticking in the sky, in the universe, on the earth, in their present city, in this particular bedroom on this extraordinary night.

The #63 Bus
from the Gare de Lyon

Paul and Letty Gerard had never been to the Père Lachaise cemetery. They'd been to Paris a hundred times—okay, maybe a dozen, once for six months, the enormous fifth floor apartment near the Parc Royale. All enough to make them feel that classic American sense of owning the city: *our town*, less sentimental than *our song* but the similar possessive—comfortable walking in the Marais, the outdoor food stands on the Rue de Rivoli, easy in the changes in the Metro, familiar with the benches near the fountain in the Place des Vosges, knowing the numbers of the bus to L'Opera or Saint Germaine des Pres. But they'd never made time for the famous cemetery where Oscar Wilde was buried, Balzac, Colette, whom Letty particularly loved—and the family joke, Paul's literary ancestor, his doppelgänger, the nineteenth-century writer Paul Gerard.

Naturally, Paris was the place for the second honeymoon, though the whole notion wasn't Paul's or Letty's. It was the kids' idea, not the first time the young out-romanticized the parents. Some *kids*, Sarah the accountant and Gabriel the poet-screenwriter, easily forty-five years between them. One was twenty-two, one twenty-three.

"Do you mind the convention, the cliché?" Paul asked her. "First honeymoons are problematic enough."

"We can finally go see Père Lachaise," Letty said. "See where your namesake is buried." She grinned in her easy way at him. Paul was the solemn one, Letty lighter-than-air, at least that was the mythology of their twenty-five-year marriage, begun right after graduation from Cornell.

"I think my grandfather's real name was Gerovsky," he said. "French immigration just got very creative. Though it's nice to have such a fancy figure behind me."

Paul Gerard had been a minor literary figure, a friend of Balzac's, of Dumas, author of histories, novels, significant enough to have a street named after him in the 15th arrondissement. None of his books had ever been translated into English.

Letty was packing, carefully, they only had a week. When the second suitcase was full she asked Paul to zip it. Sitting on it for a moment, she started to talk about another suggestion from family. "I think I probably brought up Père Lachaise and have cemeteries on the mind because of what your brother said last night."

"Andrew is an idiot," Paul said. His brother had called out of the blue to suggest that he and his wife were buying a cemetery plot and wouldn't Paul and Letty like to chip in with them. Not quite out of the blue: Paul and Andrew's parents had both died in the past two years, lung cancer, a stroke—and Paul himself had been in the hospital with an uneven heartbeat, straightened out quickly with medicine, but cautioning. In response Paul grew angry but very quiet, indeed.

It didn't come up again until they were about to land at Charles de Gaulle. Sipping the bitter airplane coffee, Paul surprised Letty, saying, "I don't seem to give a damn where I'm buried. But I've never been very good about death. I closed my eyes to my mother's condition even after she started spitting blood. And there are two or three friends I damned near deserted because I couldn't hack it, not the idea, not the reality."

Letty nodded, sitting on a yawn since the conversation was suddenly *so* serious. "Let's file it and forget it. In the unlikely event that either of us should turn out to be mortal, we'll think of something."

"Or Sarah and Gabriel will."

And that was an end to the Great Cemetery Plot Problem.

Nothing was said about Père Lachaise for the six days of mostly rain. The last morning was a gift: Paris gleamed, old-new in the rare sunshine. Paul and Letty were both great walkers: spectators at the grand theater of the Paris sidewalks. This morning it was the Isle St. Louis, walking across the Pont des Arts. They held hands as they walked. It was not because they were in Paris, it was because of where they'd been. They'd had a bad patch in their marriage, the accustomed ease of understanding giving way under the pressure of—of what? Paul turning forty, restless, the law not so engaging as it had been before he'd made partner. Letty fired in a sudden downsizing at the private school where she taught, Letty missing the children. Now they were delighted to have come out on the other side, holding hands, walking in Paris, suddenly starving for lunch.

After the second espresso, he looked at her and grinned. She understood perfectly, it was going that way these days. "It's the number sixty-three bus from the Gare de Lyon," Letty said. She'd looked it up that morning, Père Lachaise was too far for a cab and they shouldn't splurge, money was tighter than in the old days. They bought a map at the gate—all the famous names with their path and plot numbers. Letty wanted to see Colette, Paul was interested in Balzac.

Walking up the pretty planted paths, as much like a park as a cemetery, Letty said, "Colette and Balzac, we're like that old Simon and Garfunkel song where she reads her Emily Dickinson and he reads his Robert Frost."

"I remember. 'Dangling Conversation.' Very sad, very Sixties."

They found Colette's grave, modest, subtle, and could not believe that a young woman, actually wearing a hat, was kneeling by the stone monument with a little clump of flowers in her hand. It was all too perfect: the sun slipping between slight puffs of clouds, the easy breeze that hung in the leaves of the plane trees, the girl, clearly moved by her memorial mission.

"We didn't bring anything for Balzac—worse, nothing for the other Paul Gerard." She was silent for a moment as they walked on. "Maybe we *should* get a plot," she said. "So the kids won't be stuck at the last minute."

"Hey," Paul said, adept at avoidance, "here's the great man himself." Balzac towered in Rodin's stone, greatness, ambition incarnate. "Wow," Paul murmured, too impressed even to be silent. Letty, however, was so impressed her natural response was to make a joke; ever the family official jokester. "What a man," she said. "He has delusions of adequacy."

Paul was not amused at humor to topple his hero. He started to move on. Letty caught up and stepped in front of him, surprising him with a kiss, a real one, not a game.

"Don't be embarrassed. This can't be the first time people have kissed in a cemetery."

"If you stay where you are it may be the first time a man has an erection in a cemetery."

"Time will take care of that."

"*Dommage,*" he said.

Easy with each other again they idled and got lost along several branching paths. The map was no help and suddenly, around a corner, behind an enormous oak Letty saw the tallest monument thus far. The words Paul Gerard shone, large, in the sunlight, the same sunlight that now dazzled Letty's eyes, made her feel faint., immediately beyond jokes. "Paul Gerard . . ." There was Paul's name carved on the tombstone as they'd always known it was somewhere far away in France and where they'd known it was sure to be someday in America. She swayed, chilled. "Paul," she said. He took it in coolly, the noble scroll-like lettering, the dates 1813–1867, cool enough to be alert when Letty fell against him. He eased her to the ground, a resting nest of leaves, gravel and earth.

She hadn't fainted, was conscious because she said, "It's your—"

Impossibly, shadowing the moment, the sun faded into a fringe of whirling dark clouds. Without sun a chill struck the air. "Hey," Paul said. "Easy does it. Look . . ." He pointed lower down on the obelisk where, in French fashion, a photograph of the deceased was embedded. An irascible, dark middle-aged man, jowly, mordant. Paul was fair, smiles came swiftly to him. "Look," he said. "It's not me. It's him. I told you I'm nowhere near ready."

Letty managed a smile, looked up where the blackness had taken absolute control of the sky. It began to rain lightly at first. Paul pulled her up—ever cautious, even on this perfect day, he had an umbrella but there was no time to open it—and they ran for it. Buses and economy forgotten they hailed a passing cab—unusual in Paris but it was apparently not a usual day. By the time they were safely in, the skies were pouring heavy rain.

"Americains?" the cab driver asked.

"Oui."

"I 'ave nevair seen such a change. First warm, *tres doux* . . . then, in one minute freeze, cold and rain. Whoooof."

Paul held a still shaky Letty, warming her. "Sshhh. He turns out to be an awful-looking son-of-a-bitch. Sour. Probably a lousy writer. I'm disowning him. Maybe I'll change my name."

"Seeing your name . . . My God . . . on a tombstone . . . All this time imagining it, kidding around is one thing but this—" She did not look up at him. Breathing deeply as if after a run she said nothing for several long minutes. Then, "Okay, I'm okay now. But

I'm through visiting cemeteries. Except maybe one more time." She tried a smile to see how it would feel. "The only good thing about a cemetery is that when your turn finally comes—you're not there."

"You see," Paul said, rocking her a bit in his arms. "There's always a bright side." He gazed down at her huddling in the curve of his arms. "Letty," he said, "one of us has to be good about this stuff. One of us will go first, doesn't usually happen simultaneously."

"Shit," she said, all her recovered good humor gone, for the moment.

"Then don't go," Paul said, taking her role, the temporary jokester to get her through this. Then, as they arrived at their corner, "No, don't open the umbrella in here. It's bad luck."

No need; the sun sang its earlier song. Paris winked at them through a gauze of yellow haze, half wet, half sun, all shimmer and promise. They translated that promise quickly into action. They knew as they fumbled with each other's clothing, the zipper on her skirt, the buttons on his shirt, that they were acting out the convention, passion after cemeteries, love against death. But they were not acting, they were impelled, without thought, and fell in a jumble of arms and legs onto the bed; they had at that moment no desire to be original, only a desire for desire.

Afterwords, sweating in each other's arms Letty murmured, "Second Honeymoon my ass. Just like a couple of kids on their first trip to Paris."

Paul breathed deeply: happy, exhausted. Then Letty was up on one elbow looming, naked, casting a mottled erotic shadow. "Don't the French call all that 'le petit mort'?" She spoke in a little girl's voice. Paul looked up at her, curious. "Only the ecstatic climax. *C'est fort*," he said, to keep it French, to keep it light.

"Okay," Letty said. "It's all around us this 'mort.' It's fearful foolishness not to go in with your brother."

Paul rose from the damp sheets, sensing a change in the air. "Like buying land—that's all," he said. "Quite small."

176

Letty tossed him a smile. "Land we have no intention of occupying for about a hundred years."

She grabbed his waist and pulled him back to the tangle of sheets. "Let's do it!" she said.

"Again?"

"No. Let's call Andrew and tell him okay. Besides," she was able now to rescue a full laugh from the somberness of the occasion. "Besides, we've already seen your place. You've already done it once."

"Right," Paul said, "dying gets easier with practice."

Unembarrassed by nakedness, they threw open the broad casement windows. The Paris sun winked at them through trembling shadows cast by chestnut trees and glinting off the tops of still soaked taxis. In the distance Notre Dame held its terrifying counsel of faith and mortality.

"It's a shame to leave all this," Letty said, looking at the sudden gift of the fountain in the hotel courtyard and beyond it all the sunny sloping sea of mansard roofs.

"Yes," he said. "It'll be a damned shame."

In the Country
of the Young

Part One: Prelude

In my seventeenth year I yearned most desperately for sexual experience. In that same year I yearned most desperately to be free of the slightly mad dream of a musical career my obsessed family saw as my destiny. How could I have dreamed that both of these needs were to be addressed in the person of the beautiful, the magical, the sensuous Kitty James.

I was a member of the unredeemable company of adolescent sexual fanatics. Mine was a science fiction world of mouths, breasts, legs, rumps: an alternative world which I felt set me off from the rest of humankind; a freak of sexual longing, unable to turn fantasy into reality. Timid and voracious at the same time, I was not forceful in such matters. I would have sold my soul for a welcoming smile from a Sarah or a Nancy or a Nina. As for their welcoming me with open arms not to mention legs, for this I needed a female liberator. One such was on the way. Kitty James, newborn writer and an artist of mouth-to-penis resuscitation, was already packing her bags in Ravinia, a Chicago suburb, heading East, in full uniform, in quest of her—and, as it would turn out, my—salvation. A migratory bird of ambition, she flew in on the wings of her unfinished first novel, *The Body-Soul Problem*.

Young as she was—owning twenty-three years, six years older than me—Kitty gave the sense that she could do anything, and at the same time was helpless in the grip of a self she was frantically trying to know and control, a self which drove her from one mood to another, ecstatic or miserable often within minutes. At first sight she gave the impression of control, tall enough to have to wear flat heels even on formal occasions.

Of course, we were young and on the Lower East Side of New York; we had no formal occasions, we could celebrate everything. But the real cause for celebration was Kitty's arrival from another time-space continuum—the Chicago suburb where her father sold cars and her mother was on the verge of going mad.

I was on the verge of everything and nothing. I'd graduated from the High School of Music and Art a year earlier than the usual—bolstering the dangerous family notion of my incipient genius—and I cared only for my viola and girls, having no idea what to do about the rest of my life. My family, however, was absolutely certain. They were in the grip of an overriding fantasy: I was going to be a great concert artist, another Jascha Heifetz. And when my teachers switched me from the violin to the viola because violists were in short supply, they didn't miss a beat. I would be another William Primrose, the great English viola virtuoso. The dream of musical careers was the family insanity.

My father, whose family in Russia had boasted a violinist, the concertmaster, no less, in the Bolshoi Ballet orchestra, drove a taxi, sold insurance, and played pinochle for medium stakes—medium or high being anything he could not afford, which was everything. He could barely afford the two dollars a week at the Settlement School for my viola lessons with Mr. Rosanoff, that wispy, gray, tiny man who was forever tuning my viola when I wanted him only to inspire me.

My mother had a sweet singing voice along with the regret-fantasy that such a voice might have thrilled audiences given the chance fate had denied her. On the rare social occasions when family was more than just my sister and me and our parents, my mother would sing "twas on the Isle of Capri that I met her . . ." with a lovely tremolo, and you could almost believe in the fame and money that were owed her by Old Man Fate who controlled the musical and financial destinies of the world.

She concentrated on my sister's singing career—except Connie was only twelve, so her moment of truth was far off in the future. Mine, however, was almost at hand. Months before my high school graduation the previous June, my father had been after me to apply to the Curtis Institute in Philadelphia. "They have the best, the finest for the violin, Efrem Zimbalist who studied with Leopold Auer in Moscow, the same teacher as Heifetz. And Primrose who is such a player that composers write concertos just for him. If they say you have it, you have it. You'll be set for life." He'd never known a soul who was set for life, who wasn't struggling every day to get through life. Naturally the notion was immensely attractive.

I took my anxiety to Art Kohn. We were what passed for buddies though Art Kohn was utterly taciturn about sex. I don't think he had my disease: terminal shyness. For him it was more as if sex had occurred on some other planet; he'd read about it, understood it, but it was not a pressing matter for him to consider. As to the question of my famous audition, he spoke out, in his mordant manner. Disappointment was his native tongue and for good reason. Art had a dark, failed past.

"You probably won't get the audition because your Mr. Rosanoff is not a hot teacher with connections at Juilliard or someplace like that. It's bad enough he has to go to the hospital for an operation just when you need him the most. Besides," Art's pudgy face clouded, as if the man in the moon had frowned, "even if you get the audition you probably wouldn't pass. There are guys competing who have been practicing day and night since they were three."

We were the realistic generation. Only the grown-ups were held in the grip of musical romanticism: The letter from Curtis offering me an audition would come, I would play magnificently, I would be accepted, I would be launched, like a missile, towards the fabled Carnegie Hall debut. I was more realistic. I'd researched the concert world, had spoken at length to Mr. Klotzman who taught theory and had played the viola under Stokowski. "You don't know what it takes to launch a concert career. Bucks, big bucks. Leonard Rose married a wealthy woman, likewise, Joseph Shuster. Isaac Stern found an heiress in San Francisco to lease Carnegie Hall for his debut. Primrose is married to a wealthy woman. That's what it takes to get a management, to arrange tours, publicity. Behind every great artist is money. Besides, the viola is not such a hot ticket for a solo career, not like the violin or the piano. You'd better start applying to colleges, real colleges: NYU, Michigan. You've got terrific grades. Think about scholarships, a teaching career." He blew a mist of resin dust from the belly of his viola. "My God, Billy, even in an orchestra like the Kansas City Symphony these days, a full season is only six and a half months."

I explained, as well as I could, about my father's obsession. Klotzman understood. But his only advice was unusable: "Stand up to him. Tell him you started too late. That I said your musicianship is fine, lots of feeling—but your technique is not up there."

What I could not explain to him was how my own sexual madness had eaten up my will. I could oppose no one, let alone my father, Joseph Gold, famous along Second Street, celebrated along Avenue C and D, whose uncle had been concertmaster at the Bolshoi Theater in Moscow. I would go through with the audition but I applied to three colleges as well, on the chance that if Primrose turned thumbs down on my concert career, I could decide, later on, if I wanted to be the fourth from the last violist in the Kansas City Symphony, whose season was about six and a half months—leaving its musicians to fend for themselves the rest of the year. About life I was most reasonable and realistic. About my own frustrated passions I was on the moon.

The invitation to the audition not having arrived, I determined to put on only the dumb show of practicing. I was convinced that it was a hopeless charade. Even if I was offered the audition, I would play my Bach Suite, Art would accompany me in the Handel Viola Concerto and Mr. Rosanoff's arrangement of the Tchaikovsky Rokoko Variations and Primrose would turn thumbs down. I would be judged to be good but not nearly world class and my parents would at last see the light of reality. In any case, practicing would have to take a back seat since all my energies were consumed by my nonexistent, all-consuming sexual life.

Even for those more innocent days I was a slow starter. At the ripe age of sixteen and a half I was a smoldering mess of unacted sexual urges. Dangling as I was between the triumph of graduating high school early, at the top of my class, and the void of waiting for my audition, I had no idea what I wished to do with my life except play the viola in string quartets with my friends and find some way to move from masturbation fantasies and furtive touching of passing women in the street—of which more later—to The Real Thing.

My poor troubled mother, beset by ailments, many genuine, and my poor harried father with his three jobs, still falling financially behind every month—what did they know of this music and sex crazed stranger inhabiting their apartment but not their lives? My father behind the wheel of his taxi, undoubtedly bragging of his son the musician, my mother behind her cashier's apron, both assuming I was home crash-practicing seven hours a day. (Even when I did practice, I would interrupt at least once every half-hour to consider masturbating, so pressing were the sexual fantasies beneath the rhythms and runs of Handel and Bach.)

What would Joseph and Fanny Gold have said if they knew that their son the sex-maniac had taken to feigning insouciance on First Avenue and walking past women, in the guise of a vigorous walking style, arms swinging freely and casually letting his swinging hand touch a rounded rump rustling under silk as if by accident; the pleasure of that illicit touch which seemed in my self-justification to give me something precious, the feel of a woman's body, however fleeting, and yet took nothing from her. (I had often considered the subway or bus option, proximity for illicit touching being so tempting—but the danger of being caught, confronted, eye-to-eye, hand-to-buttock or thigh, seemed somehow greater.)

The street adventure was not without its own dangers but could usually be executed without the woman in question noticing— crowded times of day were best for this reason. Several times a woman had turned and nailed me with an accusing glance. I expected a scene, screams, police, even. But the yearning young must be under some special protection. No such punishments ever ensued. What my parents would have thought if they had found out was—unthinkable.

And what would my poor, gently puritanical mother have said if she knew her sensitive musician-son, instead of plugging away at the Schubert "Arpeggione" sonata, had become a virtuoso of stairs, any stairs which a woman might ascend, the long fruitful subway steps being a favorite, steps beneath which the budding adolescent voyeur could lurk, letting his apparently innocent gaze float upwards where still more innocent women in skirts and dresses moved balletically while those same skirts and dresses swirled up allowing me the glimpse of forbidden thigh, sleek or plump, pale or tanned, of white or pink or blue panties? Once the gracious gods of lust sent a fortuitous gust of wind and I actually saw a pair of blue and pink flowered panties bearing the mysterious legend Wednesday. Oh blessed Wednesday, that marvelous Wednesday morning as she'd stood by her bed, naked as Eve, pulling on those magical panties—a colorful travel brochure of a country forbidden to me, all foreign travel banned by my cursed shyness.

But this is not really to be about the strange youngster I was. It is about my guide to the country of the young, Kitty James—Kitty and her cartoon-red bow of a mouth which would soon introduce me to sex and to myself. Kitty, who would arrive to rescue the young pervert-manqué from an incorrigible shyness; a shyness which kept me on the periphery of male-female contact.

Two months before Kitty's arrival, I was suffering the prolonged tortures of "going out" with Laurel Levine, the harpist I had met at Music and Art. Only the damned can know what it means to be with a harpist who wears silk print dresses, often dragging the floor, sometimes above the knee, the promised softness of her blonde-fuzzed skin, of cheek, of arm, everything else being shielded by dresses, by scarves, a creature from another century, entirely pre-sex. Damned because IT IS IMPOSSIBLE TO MAKE A SEXUAL PASS AT A GIRL WHO PLAYS THE HARP. Don't forget it's angels who play harps, no matter how eloquent their rounded asses might be as they bend over to adjust a pedal, no matter how cruel the perfume they shed under your impassioned nose as they turn a page. You are playing, let's say, a Brahms viola sonata, the limpid piano part arranged for harp, and she sits behind that lyre-shaped anachronism, finding rolling chords to place beneath your rough viola sounds; this is not the famous perfume ad with a violinist madly kissing the pianist in the middle of the rehearsal. This is me and Laurel Levine pouring angelic song through the windows onto King's Highway in Brooklyn. It is hopeless.

Part of the curse of my taxi-driver father and cashier mother's cultural ambitions for me was that I seemed to know only such girls as played the harp, or a lutenist (even worse), and our second violinist, Masha Winkler, a Soviet-style prude who would not even let me carry her violin. I did date a poet from Canada who'd been in my class at school, a charmless blonde girl with an arctic smile who liked to indulge in long, cool Canadian kissing bouts (silently so as to not wake her sleeping parents). But never, never allowed me even an inch below the border. It was heaven and hell all wrapped up in one.

Into this prison of desire marched the army of liberation, Kitty James, actually wearing the uniform of the Women's Corps of the United States Army—not her own uniform, as I learned later—and carrying the beginning of her novel, *The Body-Soul Problem*.

Part Two: Andante Con Passione

We met at a party at Chuck Charles's place. I was, at the time, being treated by Chuck Charles, for my shyness. Chuck, a self-styled therapist who lived in a cold-water flat on Second Street off Avenue A, had convinced me that I was in no mere adolescent quandary, to be solved by time and good fortune: I had a syndrome of shyness crying out to be cured. To achieve this, he was hypnotizing me, twice a week, with not a word to my family who would have firmly shut off this fountain of nonsense. But I was sixteen and a half. I told my family nothing—or at least the minimum of what I thought they needed to know. To pay Chuck I used the money earned from small gigs, playing for modern dancers at the 92nd Street YMHA or at Hunter College auditorium. I had serious doubts about how helpful these hypnosis sessions were. But I was desperate.

The party.

First imagine a series of sawed-off tenements lining the numbered streets, in this case Second Street. Now slice an imaginary knife through the center of the buildings and see the small apartments, no windows in the interior rooms, unless they gave onto a shaft, each apartment with a bathtub in the kitchen and a tiny toilet just off the kitchen. The furniture, early nothing. Relics of an earlier time, these were called cold-water flats because there was no hot water and the bathtub had to be filled with kettles of heated water. La Bohème circa nineteen fifties, everyone busy smoking cigarettes, occasionally pot, everyone believing in the power of art, love, lust, and literature. The supporting cast: Jules Chasin, our first violinist, cool, technically brilliant, but determined to join his family's import-export business, Boris Bruner our cellist, Brooklyn-toughened, sardonic, already settled into an affair with a Polish nurse at New York Hospital, and Chuck Charles, half charlatan, half intense researcher into hypno-therapy.

Against this backdrop I was to play my shy Rodolfo and Kitty her slightly mad Mimi.

When I knocked, Kitty James opened the door, a khaki jacketed and skirted surprise—tall, WASPy blonde hair, green eyes and wearing the uniform of the Women's Army Corps which I thought had been disbanded years before.

"Hello," she said, "I'm Kitty James, I'm in from Chicago, this is actually my sister's uniform from the Women's Army Corps and I'm writing a novel and I had an affair with a major novelist who taught me several sexual special tricks and I'm determined to get my novel finished, published, and famous if I have to hole up here with Chuck for the next ten years. And while this is happening I will demonstrate occult ways for my mouth and body's center to speak to your body and soul's deepest center otherwise known as your penis, and we will have a long and complicated connection with a surprising denouement."

Of course she said nothing like that, those phrases being the subtext of what luck and destiny were to provide. I have no recollection of what she actually said. Her physical presence, a sensuality emphasized by the contrast of an army uniform, her perfectly oval face, bright red lips against pale skin and an intense emotional tone concealed beneath a cool smile—a movie with the sound off, the camera zooming in on the female star, with the background music soon to begin.

I think what I said was something as cloddish as, "Are you in the army?"

I held my breath after the first instant. She smelled like flowers, though I learned quickly that she never used perfume or cologne. The scent was extra—unexpected, like Kitty.

"No," she said, leaving it at that.

The evening was hers. Jules suspended plans to play Haydn and Mozart quartets and serenaded her with Paganini caprices played with seductive virtuosity. Boris Bruner forgot his Polish nurse long enough to sit on the floor next to Kitty and offer her a joint. Even the cool silent Masha, having few words, showed Kitty the violin she'd smuggled out of the Soviet Union. Art Kohn watched and waited.

Chuck Charles was, as well as an alternative psychotherapist, a collector of strays. I was one such stray, even though I still lived with my father, mother, and sister only two blocks away. Kitty was Chuck's newest charge. At one point in the evening he raised his plastic glass of Gallo red and toasted her. "To Kitty, whose novel will finally solve the oldest problem in philosophy: the soul-body problem."

As taken with her as the rest, I was instantly jealous of Chuck, a feeling which lasted until a much later Kitty-conversation replaced it with a worse feeling. I asked her how she could stay, comfortably, in Chuck's apartment when I was now her lover.

"Chuck is homosexual. Didn't you know?"

Know? Of course not. I had a vague horror of the notion. The only thing more terrifying to me than heterosexuality was its opposite. Undoubtedly everyone at the party knew about Chuck except me. In any case no one cared about much except loosening up with wine and pot and Kitty James.

Kitty got bombed easily; or she may have arrived slightly smashed. To everyone's dismay—including mine—she glommed onto me, unutterably moved by what Chuck had told her about my as yet mythical audition. "I'm going to come to Carnegie Hall when you play there."

"Well . . ."

"And I expect a free ticket . . ."

As usual I felt like a fraud. Not only was Carnegie Hall bullshit but there would probably not even be an audition. Fortunately Kitty had other things pressing her attention. She had never seen Central Park, we must go up to Central Park at once, leaving her other conquests strewn on the raffia matting in various states of semiconsciousness and longing. Except for Art Kohn, who sat in his chubby chair and gazed at our departure with a mysterious, patient smile. Mystery, patience, that was Art Kohn; as well as an uncanny ability to hold a room of friends in a silent trance while he played the Waldstein Sonata of Beethoven. Broke as everyone was, there was always a piano for Art Kohn to play, wherever we were: even Chuck had an upright.

Either it was summertime, or in the country of the young it is always summer; memory refuses to serve, choosing rather to lead, to replace, to invent. But it is clear that I took my viola along and, seated on a grassy slope near the fountain in the park, I took it out from its sheltering case (instead of what I *really* wished to take out). I played the beginning of the G Major Bach Suite for Kitty James. There were a million sexual narratives in my free-floating fantasy and one of them was that I would play the viola for a woman and she would instantly be ready to make love, helpless before this viola-sensuality. When I finished and laid the viola on the grass, I was quickly in the middle of a daring first kiss, breathing her flowery smell in along with the damp August park air. It seemed as if my fantasy was about to become real—but at the wrong time and in the wrong place.

189

Perhaps even with the wrong girl because the kiss seemed to be only a cue for Kitty to start to disrobe, not so much in passion as in rage. In a drunken fury she threw off her khaki skirt, started to rip off her blouse (or was it a shirt?) muttering: "Damned uniform . . . not mine, anyway . . . my sweet, goody-sister Joanie . . . right size . . . wrong girl . . . Joanie belongs . . . always belonged . . . fucking lower middle class dreams . . . the army . . . a nurse . . . Goddamn Florence Nightingale . . ."

By now she was down to her bra and panties and they were about to join the army remnant sale on the grass. "Come here, Billy," she said, stretched out, a Venus on the grass, drunken anger slipping into drunken sexual tenderness. "Come on," she murmured. I slid down next to her in a panic. My desperation, my sexual longing, was fighting with terror of a passing police car's headlights that would reveal Billy Gold with a naked woman and a viola in Central Park. But the conflict was easily resolved. When I touched her damp breast it was rising and falling with a steadiness that could only mean sleep not passion.

At twenty to three in the morning I cautiously turned the key in the door to my parents' apartment and led Kitty to the couch, no sheets not even a blanket. She was asleep at once without a mutter as was I, on the cot set up for me in the living room. (My sister Connie, on beginning her period at eleven—our family did everything early— had been awarded the second bedroom.)

In the early light I woke to whispered voices in the kitchen—the unlikely whispering duet of my father and Kitty. I crept near enough to hear my father.

". . . a Carnegie debut and then you need a manager for the tours . . . London, Paris, Rome . . . But first you need the stamp of approval from a great teacher . . . do you take sugar, milk . . . ? Heifetz had

Leopold Auer, people brought their children from all over the world . . . He said thumbs down or thumbs up . . . you were broken or you were made . . . Billy will have Primrose, the great violist from London, England . . . now at the Curtis Institute in Philadelphia . . . be set for life . . ."

I could not stand my eavesdropping role and presented myself in the kitchen doorway. My father, still in his bathrobe, was at the stove pouring coffee.

"Good morning," I said. Kitty turned her gaze from my father to me. I blazed in the glow of that glance. She saw me, years hence, no doubt wearing white tie and tails onstage, accepting the raging applause of an audience. My God, I thought, she believes all his bull-shit! What is it about music that makes people check their brains at the door? No one would see an easel and a paintbrush and dream of anything but hardship, poverty and neglect. But mention a concert career and people buy every movie cliché and are ready for their free ticket to Carnegie Hall. My father and Kitty were soul mates, companions in fantasy.

The next day Art Kohn and I met at our usual hangout, the Carnegie Tavern, around the corner from Carnegie Hall, where for the price of a dark German beer you could sit forever—if you could convince the waiter you were eighteen. Jules and Boris Bruner would join us later, after a record date—a French conductor was in town and cutting a record and Boris's father who was part French knew someone in the conductor's family: thus Boris had gotten the gig and had worked Jules in, too. This was the contingent universe we inhabited, lucky one day, nothing the next.

We were neither country rats with village and rural wisdom, nor were we truly city rats, smug with street smarts. We were Music and Art rats: we knew the streets, especially the Lower East Side, but also the sleek streets just south of Carnegie Hall, gleaming with well-dressed, expensive women, fresh from shopping at Bergdorf's, leafing through folders of sheet music for their children's piano lessons at Patelson's Half Price sheet music shop on 56th Street, across from the tavern, or having lunch in the dining rooms of hotels—no one we knew had ever stayed overnight in a hotel—smiling at each other with the glamour of women who knew they could kindle desire by merely existing. Streets dotted with close-shaven men in dark suits—none of our fathers wore suits except at weddings or bar mitzvahs—these were men who walked with purpose, striding, men who had places to get to, the problem of where to *want* to go long since resolved—not grazing their surfaces as we did, glued to our instruments like Siamese twins, lounge lizards of the asphalt.

We knew the Metropolitan Museum, claimed the Museum of Modern Art as our own, playing the game of pontificating over favorite paintings, fancying that our status as musicians gave us special rights in the matter of all art: Rembrandt up, Corot down, de Chirico, my haunting favorite, long sunlit Italian vistas of a surreal Italy all sun and shadows. Like most young people we fled our parent's home, we were outside-rats (long before malls) and the sidewalks kept us pure, neutral, uncommitted. Still, we needed tables where for the price of a beer or a coffee we could nest, take apart our experiences, our desires and disappointments and glue them back together with our sticky hopes. Rare and lucky are the grown-ups, the adults who have the place of pause, the oasis of time and space, correcting the headlong pace of the day, the place that youth naturally finds and makes its own.

My sexual adventures, my experiments with the perversions of illicit touching and secret spying, these were the solitary underside of this group life. When I came up for air I wanted to be with the music-rats.

"She's weird, this Kitty."

"How do you mean?"

"She crosses her fingers a lot."

It was the kind of thing Art would do, watch the newcomer who was setting everybody on fire to catch her in some oddball behavior. "I also think I saw her knock on wood a few times when she was talking about this book she's writing."

"A few superstitions, everybody has some of those."

"I'd watch out," Art said darkly. "There's something strange about her. She could be dangerous."

Strange was a word made for Art. Detached, Olympian, having nothing to lose since he had already lost everything, he walked alongside us or sat opposite in a booth at the Carnegie Tavern, a glass of dark German beer for company, astonishing in his absence. Everyone knew he had played at the Salle Pleyel in Paris when he was eight, the Mozart Twenty-Fourth Concerto, Mitropolous conducting, before drying up, years later, after high school, giving his doting mother a nervous breakdown, his father long since dead. He never spoke of it, but his inability to perform in public anymore sat next to him, a pale but constant shadow, as much his companion as we were. Art was all vanished past and suspended future, no present. Even when he played, he was a ghostly figure. If, on occasion, he laughed wildly without control, it seemed like a surreal laugh, as if he was remembering something secretly funny, not the meager humor that had just been offered.

After Kitty had practically dragged me and my viola out to Central Park in the middle of the night, one would expect a friend to ask, "Did you make it?" Or the gross but more precise, "Did you get in?" Which was precisely what Jules asked when he and Boris arrived. At which I unfolded the night, the frantic stripping of the uniform as police cars rolled by, the sudden narcoleptic sleep which aborted the promise of sex.

I told them everything. I had no feeling of disloyalty to Kitty.

Those were innocent days, lust, affection and infatuation living comfortably side by side with the camaraderie of young men. One did not betray the other. There was no forbidden knowledge, only shared experience, the information of our souls. We ended that particular day walking across the Brooklyn Bridge to where Boris lived, Art Kohn chanting Hart Crane: *"What mere toil could align thy choiring strings . . ."*

Later, at Boris's house, getting into the Kitty act, Boris took me aside. Touching his finger to his nose, both sly and solemn, he said, "Listen, Billy, you know there's one place on a woman's body, the clitoris, once you get to touch it, they go wild, it's all over, she's yours. It's magic, you can't lose." I took this wisdom seriously. After all this was Boris who was always slipping away with his cello to New York Hospital where he and his nurse would do it endlessly, according to his cool-voiced reports. To clinch his argument he pulled out a book by Havelock Ellis and showed me a schematic drawing, locating the seat of magic for me. He also showed me the entry under Cunnilingus. Convinced, Machiavellian, I made my plans.

Later when Art and I played the main audition piece for the group, the one I was preparing for Primrose, the Handel Concerto, all I could think about was Kitty—the real audition I yearned for was still to come. Soon, I devoutly hoped.

Chuck Charles had met some guy and was shacking up with him for the duration. He came by and left Kitty a key and instructions for heating the bathtub water. Kitty was, in the meantime, preparing to initiate me into the mysteries of sex.

"But the auguries have to be right."

Art had been right on the money. This was my introduction to her utter commitment to the varied superstitions which guarded her safety. You didn't knock on wood to make sure something bad didn't happen, you knocked twice, once with each hand. If something was truly threatening, you had to knock three times with each hand. I had no idea what "auguries" were. I just wanted them to be right so we could move on. Especially now that she had the apartment to herself. I told her about Chuck Charles's experiments with hypnosis. Her small smile registered a confidence: she could do better than mere hypnosis.

As it turned out a birthday could be an augury—as could receiving an encouraging, handwritten rejection note from *The Partisan Review*. The two coming together was cause for dinner by candlelight in her cold-water flat, Kitty, her out-of-date army uniform put aside, this night all pale colors, flat heels on beige shoes, pearls, a beige silk blouse.

She had planned, had orchestrated everything: a mind-movie directed by Kitty James, starring herself and her young virginal genius. Kitty believed in genius; she believed in futures. As for me, I believed in Kitty. It was irrelevant if I was shy or bold. It would be better than hypnosis. She took charge. "First, play that Bach piece you started in the park." I placed my viola under my chin and began. There has always been something strange about playing music for one person—unless that person is your teacher. Enclosed in a room, the player is exhibiting something to the solo listener, perhaps entreating, perhaps more aggressive than that, asking, telling, demanding response. When the response came I was ready.

I have no memory of how the clothes came off, where the instrument went; all I can testify to is the result: that we lay, naked, on the narrow cot Chuck had provided for Kitty. Even in Chuck's absence his bed was his own. The cot, like me, was virginal. Kitty, as part of her staging, had turned the lights off. I would have preferred a thousand watts, a ceiling full of eyes, of spotlights. But I was still too shy to make demands; I was to be the recipient of joy, a birthday boy unwrapping his present. I had to make do with the dim but thrilling sight of a shadowy Kitty, modest breasts, as it turned out, long legs parting, her hands more active, even, than my own. She was lavish, golden, all things gratuitous and good. Her thighs were generous, like her mouth, a double Cupid's bow happily offering kiss upon kiss.

As nervous at my good fortune as I had been about my endless frustrations, nevertheless, I had my own secret plan. Guided by Boris Burner's clitoris-revelations and the drawings in Havelock Ellis, I couldn't wait to hurl myself down—I had no idea, then, that it was actually called "going down." To me it was all ascension.

Once there, I thrilled myself by parting more veils of flesh than I'd ever dreamed existed and proceeded to my feast. But hunger did not suffice. From above me Kitty murmured, "No, no . . . No, don't bite." She gave a shivery laugh. "You've got me all wet then you breathe on me and give me a chill . . ."

I was humiliated. And now that the chips were down everything else was too; my faithful companion in solitude, my erection, deserted me, collapsed in shame. I remember thinking, "What a birthday!" even though the actual day was the following Wednesday when my parents had planned a different kind of party with quite different presents in mind. By the time I had taken my impulsive dive, the months, maybe years of outlaw touching, of outlaw peering under subway stairs—all had vanished. I was Billy Gold in bed with a lovely, willing woman and it was utterly natural and had been so since the beginning of time. But we all know what pride precedes. It is the story that has seemed to repeat itself through the years—you long, you receive, you screw up.

But Kitty would not let me be miserable even for a moment on my birthday. I was, after all, her protégé; she had decided to shepherd me, to nurse me into the greatness that would be my shining musical career. She eased herself down and lay sideways, her head opposite my shrunken penis. "Listen," she said, gazing up at me. "This is no big deal."

And with that she knelt on the bed and took me into her mouth, performing one of the immemorial acts of human connection. Who was that spiritual adventurer who first connected the lips, the mouth, the tongue to the penis? An act equal to the invention of an entire language? Who was the first woman to taste the salt of life and either spit it out or take it into herself? Paleolithic? Greek? Roman?

I present this memory in praise of the union of mouth and genitalia, giving to the human mouth its place of honor; it is, after all, the home of words, of sound, adjacent to the realm of thought, a servant of the realm of thought. (How can I know who I am until I think? How can I know what I think until I've shaped the words and spoken them?) The mouth is the natural home of ambition, of wisdom and foolishness, of the compression of experience we call wit. The lower half is mute, animal—repeating the ancient gestures of intercourse . . . the very word is abstract. *Inter—course*. Between bodies?

When Kitty's lips had almost completed their loving tour, creating as a byproduct an erection of stone, of iron, I recovered my will. I pulled her up and kissed that wide happy mouth in gratitude. I knew what to do with such a birthday gift. To keep it you had to give it back. When it was over, probably like every male virgin before me, I was unable to believe my good fortune and was astonished that it was gone. The absence of sexual pleasure after tasting it is entirely different than the endless absence before.

Almost at once Kitty wreathed the narrow bed in cigarette smoke. "This'll be good luck for my book and for your audition. The auguries are good."

Silence. Smoke. Peace. Or so I misread the moment. Then: "You know what puzzles me the most?"

"What?"

"Why is there something instead of nothing?" She turned a wide gaze at me. "To my professor it was just a problem in philosophy—Wittgenstein. But it's haunted me ever since. *Why is there something instead of nothing?* There could have been nothing. With or without a God. But somehow there's something. Why? The rock bottom question. It's like the body-soul problem. Where does one stop and the other begin?" A beat. "I'm not sure I can finish my book without knowing the answers."

I took her in. Her eyes were closed. I could feel the change in emotional temperature, she was dropping fast. "Sometimes," she said, "sometimes there is nothing, very quickly." The atmosphere was now zero or below. A sudden storm of weeping shook Kitty and I held her until the weather changed. Already I knew her well enough to know storms would come and go swiftly. She rolled on her side, a pale pink nipple winking at me in the dim light, and kissed me. "And you, young Billy," she said. "What do you think about nothing versus something?"

Without thinking I spoke my truth. "I'm just glad there's you and not nothing."

She settled down into my arms as if she lived there. "Very flattering. And don't forget the auguries," she said. "Never forget the auguries."

Part Three: Allegro Molto

The next day a letter from the Curtis Institute arrived: I had been granted an audition on August 20th. If the audition was graded PASS then I would be accepted as a student in the fall. Kitty took immediate credit, ignoring the fact that the letter had been mailed before her kiss of fire had taken place. Once again she knew better: auguries were apparently worth their weight in gold.

My mother cooked around the clock for my second birthday party—the family was naturally entirely unaware of the first—which was instantly transformed into a premature victory celebration. It was an orgy of self-satisfaction, made tolerable only by my sister Connie's beautiful singing of Faure's "Après Une Rêve," Art Kohn making the awful upright Sohmer piano sound mellifluous, French. Later, drinking some sort of weird punch my mother had concocted, I heard Kitty telling my father, "My family has no ambitions, not for themselves, not for their children. There wasn't a book in the house except for Reader's Digest Condensed Books, every magazine in the world."

"What does your father do?"

"Sells cars and drinks. Watches television, has affairs."

He patted her shoulder with the compassion of a man who understands the awfulness of growing up in a family without a musical destiny.

Still later, high on whatever was in that punch, I thought I heard my mother say to Kitty, "If you want to be a good angel, make sure he practices for his audition."

Kitty to my sister Connie: "You sing like an angel."

Connie to Kitty: "As soon as I start high school I'll stop taking lessons."

"Why?"

"You don't know this family."

For the next few weeks I was supposed to be on a frantic practicing binge. Instead I faked everyone out, including Kitty. It helped that Mr. Rosanoff was having some mysterious operation that old people have—he must have been easily fifty-one or -two. Kitty was on a binge of her own. Days were consumed by working on her novel. "My only way not to go crazy." I asked to read—anything. She refused. "I can't dilute the magic," she said.

Nights were consumed quite differently. We made love in ways even I'd never imagined, and in strange places: once in a phone booth; one evening, in a restaurant, when we were the last people there and our waiter was reading a newspaper waiting for us to leave, she slipped under the tablecloth—even the inexpensive restaurants seemed to have tablecloths in those young middle-class days. I felt privileged by danger, even though she was the active one and I usually passive.

Art Kohn got me a gig at the 92nd Street Y playing for a dancer named Katherine Litz. "God," Kitty said, "how she moves. I wonder if they call her Kitty for short." She had come to listen and look, inspired to see the creation of her "auguries" playing in the pit below the stage—even if it wasn't Carnegie Hall. During a fifteen-minute break she grabbed my hand and pulled me into a phone booth for a renewal of our sacred mysteries.

Was she crazy or just incorrigibly young? A little of each, I think. I was in love with sex, my newly discovered way to connect. In the meantime her mouth made its lyrical protestations and being inside the center of her was almost like resting from a different sort of storm.

I told her about my secret lustful life pre-Kitty, the fake swinging of arms to get a fleeting touch of woman. She thought it was hilarious, prompted me to walk with her and try it, so she could see. My heart pounding I found a young woman arms full of packages. As I began my swinging Kitty shouted, "He touched me, this boy touched me." We fled, she was shaking with laughter, I was rocked by the beating in my chest and the excitement of a grown woman knowing my secrets.

A few nights later, half asleep she turned to me and said, "Is this okay?"

"Hmmm?"

"My playing Colette to your Cheri?"

I had no idea what she meant, was no great reader of books, not really much of a student, had manufactured good grades by a kind of quick-witted mimicry and a gift for memorization. Sight-reading quartet music since I was eleven had made me good at sight-reading everything, from assigned readings in chemistry to essay questions on exams. I read books, novels, poetry, but I read them as if they were music, floating in and out of them, retaining little except their song. Once a friend's mother gave me a copy of the maxims of La Rochefoucauld. They came in handy when I wished to appear dry, cynically sophisticated with girls—with the usual miserable results.

"Colette who?" I asked.

"An older woman with a young boy. I mean you're just starting out and me with my no-holds-barred stuff."

"Everything we do is great," I said. Then, a fake shy grin. "Somebody had to be the first, show me the ropes."

She lit another of her innumerable cigarettes and, reflective, murmured, "I know a girl who likes to have men come on her breasts."

I wasn't sure what I thought about that little number so I said, "Would you like that?"

"I don't know," she said, thoughtful. Then she turned to me in that way she had of propping up on an elbow and pausing before saying something she wanted me to take really seriously. She said: "Love is a seamless web, a single feast, everything's on the dinner. But not with sex. It's all a la carte." Kitty James, my Confucius, my inscrutable La Rochefoucauld of the life of passion.

I was on the knife-edge of excitement—but I was also scared.

I could remember the Billy Gold who swung his arms in faux insouciance and lurked beneath subway steps, a Jack the Ripper of the upward gaze, all frustrated longing. I remembered him, but I no longer recognized him. Not only had that Billy Gold been a prisoner of shyness—women were like a race of Martians who could not be touched and could barely be spoken to—he'd also been a prisoner of a world of bar lines.

Nothing is as confining as the bar lines of a piece of music, a beat one marches to, even allowing for slowing down, speeding up, for syncopation—it's 4/4 or 6/8 and that's that! The playing of music opens you up—but in an ordered way, imprisoned behind bars, and this imprisonment, as passionately as that other Billy Gold had accepted it, was a part of the confinement essential to Joseph Gold's life-plan for his son. That Billy Gold had been split down the middle: part obedient musical martyr, marching towards a destiny he didn't want, part rebel of the streets and nights, longing for a freedom he couldn't quite imagine.

Kitty imagined it for me. She was like an improvisation introduced in the middle of this order: a jazz riff in the midst of a Mozart sonata, inventive, unpredictable, unrestrained by limits or by anything except the urges the mind granted the body. There was no going back—I was where I was now, fortunate, fearful—tied anxiously to this young woman who was so concerned about why there is something instead of nothing.

May was coming to an end. My mother had already picked out what I was to wear at the audition: a blue serge suit, white shirt and striped blue and red tie—and a truly exotic touch, loafers with tassels. Even the inscrutable Art Kohn was getting nervous. My teacher, Mr. Rosanoff, was back from the hospital, thin, looking even shorter than before, if that was possible, this aging elf of the viola. He listened to where I was in my audition pieces, shook his head gnomically and puffed on his pipe. Then he took up his own instrument, tuned it at excruciating length, at last, and showed me how to phrase the slow movement of the Handel Concerto so that it would break anyone's heart. The problem was, he showed me how he could do it, not how I could do it myself.

"The viola," he said between pipe puffs, "sings in the middle voice, close to the human voice. So when you go up in the higher registers you must not strain, just sing. You'll be tense at your audition. Try to sing." I would try, though my doubts were considerable.

"Just sit there," Kitty said. "Let me handle it."

"If somebody comes in—"

"Art's standing guard."

"My God."

My audition was to take place in fifteen minutes. We were in the men's room on the first floor of the Curtis Institute, home of Efrem Zimbalist, who had studied with Leopold Auer in Moscow, of Gregor Piatigorsky from Kiev, of William Primrose of London, England, for whom William Walton had written his viola concerto—I knew the entire litany from my father's endless recitations—and Kitty was going down on me, actually *up* on me right now since she was crouching at my feet as I sat on a commode, as usual terrified and thrilled.

She had insisted on coming along, fine with me. The train to Philadelphia was an adventure; the farthest I'd been from downtown or midtown Manhattan had been 135th Street and Convent Avenue, up the enormous daily hill from the subway to the High School of Music and Art. I was glad of Kitty's company on the adventure. Besides, she was bubbling with hope while Art's silence implied his usual vision of disaster on the way.

She'd worked some of her magic on Art while we rumbled through New Jersey, drawing him out about what happened to his concert career, why his mother had had a breakdown, all that verboten stuff. Amazingly he opened up to her, she was like that, impossible to hold off. Art distracted her from her more intrusive questions by telling her what it felt like to be onstage at the Salle Pleyel, adjusting the piano stool while Mitropolous waited, baton dangling, how he'd wanted to vomit, how he'd known at that moment that he would never do this again. Kitty was dazed with borrowed glamour. Not so dazed, though, that she wasn't up for the pre-audition adventure in the men's room.

Surprising me, again, she stopped just before I could come. Gazing up at me, she asked, "Billy, have you ever thought about where the body and the soul meet?"

"What? . . ."

"Is this one of the places? Or is it a time. Is this one of the times?"

I heard a bright whistle, a signal from Art Kohn our sentinel. Someone might be joining our little party. Kitty rose, as startling as when she'd suddenly knelt.

I was as dismayed by her sudden stopping as I was by the starting of the whole adventure.

I said, "But—"

"Hemingway says coming is bad before you have to perform."

"He probably meant that about writing."

"Same thing. This was just a good luck wish." She knocked on the wooden toilet seat twice with each hand and stood up.

Suddenly, echoing loud and cold in the tile walls of the bathroom, someone was playing the Bach Chaconne. We both scurried into a semblance of neatened clothing. I gestured to Kitty, turned-upward palms and a grimace which said: my God, what do we do now? She grabbed my viola with one hand, me with the other and led us past the young violinist, feverishly practicing, his hair flared over his closed eyes, a sweaty handkerchief tucked into his collar. I'm pretty sure he didn't even notice us—particularly Kitty—so engrossed was he in what was probably his last-minute warm-up session before his audition. Except that Kitty couldn't resist. "Nice tone," she said just as we were out the door.

I believe I am the first person in the history of music to play an audition with a full-blown erection. You'd think anxiety would have acted like a cold shower. But no! It was the first time the Handel Concerto was ever played with an organ accompaniment. Shaky with unsatisfied desire I concentrated on turning the viola into the human voice, as Mr. Rosanoff had taught. Primrose, tall, slender, elegant as a flower, asked polite questions between pieces and gave no clue as to success or failure. Most importantly, he never seemed to glance below my waist. I heard, years later, that he'd gone quite deaf and had to give up his concert career.

On the train back we got happily stoned on beer after beer. Exuberance, relief that it was over, elation. But the beer took Kitty down not up. She told us about her mother whose breakdowns ruled the family's schedules for years; her older sister joining the army to get away, it was Kitty who stayed, consoling her drinking father. "I was going to write a novel called 'Taking Mother Away.' Each chapter a different breakdown." Rain began to wash the windows and Kitty stared through them like a heroine in an old movie.

"My mother, too," Art said. He'd never said a word about that before, though we all knew his mother was in what Jules called "some Laughing Academy up in Westchester." By the time we hit New York Art and Kitty were trading histories and emotions. She offered him her Wittgenstein puzzler: why is there something instead of nothing?

"I've tried nothing," she said. "Twice. It would be really something to be able to test nothing against something."

"I don't think it works that way," Art said. "Once you give up the something you can't get back to it."

She nodded, solemn. Did she know what he meant? Did he know

what she meant? It sounded like gibberish to me, but of course they'd each had more of a life than I had, which meant large-sized disappointments I could not fathom. Was she talking about suicide attempts? Whatever the subject matter, they seemed to be on the same wavelength. I was oddly detached, immune to jealousy. Staring into my beer I prayed that I would not be accepted, I worked on my speech to my parents about college, about the joys of a liberal arts degree, about playing the viola for pleasure not to conquer the world. I was seventeen, entrapped in my skin and my self-conscious soul. Others were, for the moment, a mysterious, distant road to knowledge.

Part Four: Finale

In those days letters had the aura of destiny. Long before faxes or e-mail, letters told of being drafted into the army, of being accepted or rejected by this or that college. Long distance telephone calls were for emergencies. For tragedies there were telegrams, yellow messengers of death. But the envelope in the mailbox was what said yes or no to hopes.

You can imagine the scenes after the "no" letter arrived, the letter which ended the charade of my adolescence. My father treated me as if I had contracted a mysterious illness, my mother turned her attentions instantly to Connie, planning the future my sister despised. But life went on as did love. When I told them about the acceptance by Michigan, of my full tuition scholarship, it was treated as a flight, the way my grandparents had fled the anti-Semitism of Russia. I was not accused of failure, only of bad luck.

Not so with Kitty. Instead of sympathy, anger; she confused me with fate. We both had failed her. The auguries had not come through. She abandoned me, refused to see me, to answer my phone calls. Strangely, what I missed most was not the astonishing sexual attentions which had ended my belated innocence. I missed the play of fantasy, her wild mood swings, the often inappropriate laughter, her superb superstitious hope which informed every action, which, at every turn, invested a random universe with meaning.

I never even got to tell her I had failed. Boris Bruner told Jules, Jules told Chuck Charles who told Kitty. I *wanted* the scene, the hysterical, reproachful scene that would at least put a full stop to the extended romance with a fantastical future. It finally came, but not in the way I'd expected.

Entering Art Kohn's dark, scrungy, furniture-packed apartment one day to pick up the piano scores from my audition—I'd rung the doorbell a hundred times with no response—I heard mumbling sounds from the one bedroom in the back. and there, a half-dressed Art Kohn lay on his unmade bed, Kitty crouched between his legs. At the same instant in which I prepared myself to receive my astonishment at the sight, I thought, swiftly, *of course*, remembering the long suddenly intimate exchanges on the train to Philadelphia, Art onstage, waiting for Mitropolous to start the orchestral introduction to the Brahms Second Concerto, a new Art, ready for Kitty to vet a return to his musical destiny—both of them sickeningly at home with the idea that instead of something there could be nothing.

This sounds all very grand and lyric inside my head. But what actually came out was, "Shit!"

Kitty raised her head apparently unsurprised, as if she had been expecting me to interrupt and afford her the scene, the high moment of reproach and explication. She was still holding Art's saddened prick in her hands and, without missing a beat began, "My God, what did you expect? You were my hope," she said. "Not just my luck, my hope." Art tried to scramble out of the scene, to make himself invisible, but Kitty held on to his prick as if it gave her the strength to continue. "What did you expect?" Her face crumpled, an exquisite oval distorted by a grimace of tears. *"Did you think I could live without hope?"*

She was right. I should have expected something like this. She had come to New York, wearing a fake uniform and bearing an incomplete novel which might or might not exist, carrying some sad, sacred knowledge earned by her extra six years on earth, a knowledge unknown to the immature natives she would meet. She believed in The Country of the Young; she was not equipped to deal with failure—while I, I had half-expected it from the start, felt it as a kind of success, a freedom.

In the instant it took for me to back out of that bedroom apartment the feelings delayed by shock arrived—a sickening sense of betrayal oddly mixed with gratitude, something it would have been ludicrous to try to express but which lurked in my trembling stomach, in my heart's uneven pulsing. Gratitude at being introduced to the life of impulse, never again to be so unconfined, so unconcerned with limits or propriety, that life of uninhibited impulses never again to be so purely itself. She could mouth the penis of everyone in the quartet, of every man in New York, and it would not spoil my gratitude.

Then I went home and threw up.

Part Five: Coda

As it turned out Kitty bet wrong—put her money on the wrong piano. She was heroic, got Art to try, to talk to managers, to play auditions. But when the chips were down, he was still Art, gifted but unable to give up the past, the boy standing, terrified, on the stage in Paris knowing he was in the wrong place and would never in his life do it again.

While I, if I've not had the career my father and mother or Kitty would have chosen for me, I have at least found a middling place in the musical world; light years from my father's dreams of glory, but something, not nothing. My quartet, the Guadanini Quartet, is in its nineteenth year, named for the instruments my father-in-law Lawrence Levitas, the mattress king, donated at an approximate cost of two and a half million dollars. I have indeed played in Carnegie Hall, though only once and, of course, I had to share the glory four ways. My sister Connie was in the middle of a tricky pregnancy and couldn't come; however, my mother wept, happy, my father played impresario with orchestra tickets for a half-dozen friends. "The viola," he lectured them during intermission, "is the glue that holds quartet music together."

No one could know, least of all my Mycaenas of a father-in-law, that the quartet would never make it to the first rank: no Juilliard, no Guarneri, no Tokyo, no world tours; that we would find a modest nest at Case Western Reserve as quartet-in-residence, teaching most of the academic year, with an annual, tiny spring tour of the smaller cities, those spurned by the big quartets. Susie stays with our son and daughter for those ten short days.

It all began to turn around in my third year at Michigan. I was on a second date with shy, delicate Susie Levitas. Over dinner, on a roll of reminiscence, risking any chances I might have of making my way with Susie, I told her about Kitty, ending with the famous night in Central Park, I told her the way playing the Bach Suite cinched the seduction, though it was unclear who was seducing whom.

"Did she ever publish that book?" Susie asked, a quiet girl of the present asking about a tornado of the past.

"I'm not sure there ever was a book." I'd never admitted that to myself until then. "She invented herself. That didn't work so she tried to invent me."

Susie came back to my room and asked me to play for her, competing, perhaps, with the ghost she'd just heard of. I'd never left my viola behind, played in the school orchestra and, incorrigibly hooked, wove the viola into my life at Ann Arbor. I played the same Bach G Major Suite I'd played for Kitty—with a similar result. I, Kitty-trained, older, was now the bold one. Susie was profoundly shy—daughter of a brash business-king. She didn't tell me about how much money her family had until she invited me to meet her family in Shaker Heights—her family being two sisters and a father, Lawrence Levitas, whose fortune had been made on the mattress slogan *Don't Just Sleep—Levitate on a Levitas.*

Levitas had wanted to be a concert pianist but fortune dictated not moving people with music but putting them to sleep in comfort. Susie now presented the old man with a prospective son-in-law who would be his newest enterprise: backing and launching an entire string quartet. No shy flower, unlike his daughter, Levitas wanted to name it the Levitas Quartet. It took months of lobbying to convince him to name it after the magnificent instruments he would buy for us.

Did I tell you that Boris Bruner and Jules Chasin joined us once when the University launched a Schubertiad? We did the Octet. But this is not to say that anything like the early days prevail. We are all older, we have our place in the world, our obligations, tenure, homes, incomes.

Still, safe in the harbor of middle-class middle age, having long forgotten those early dreams of glory—dreamt for me only by others—I have never quite forgotten my slightly mad princess of the irreplaceable country of the young. That country whose borders are years, whose population is uncountable, whose principal products are hope, ambition and despair, a country whose natural condition is civil war and which once left is utterly lost: that country of the young, whose borders, once passed, remain forever closed, and which haunts everyone in the Diaspora of encroaching age with the impossibility of return. We are young, for a time, and when that is taken from us we accept in exchange a gift of memory.

It's tempting to use the passport of remembrance, to revisit my seventeenth year. Still, it's hard work for memory to evoke the distant life of cold-water flats, the dazed exaltation of weekend marathons playing Mozart, Schubert, Debussy, Bartok nonstop for forty-eight hours as if time-constraints and sleep-needs apply only to the adult, nonmusical world, players dropping in and out, sleeping on couches, on floors, music-rats, street-rats-city-rats, exiles from the safe havens of our families, citizens of the night air, no past, no future, all present.

And to remember Kitty and me in our narrow bed, and my innocent birthday gift of blonde sensuality from that passionate, confused mouth, that mouth which taught me that there are no boundaries separating the body and the soul, and how important it is, how happy we should be—*pace* Wittgenstein—that there is, after all, something instead of nothing.

Melissa Branfman

DANIEL STERN is the author of nine novels and three other story collections. In 1990 Stern's *Twice Told Tales* won the Rosenthal Foundation Award given by the American Academy of Arts and Letters. He's been at various times in his working life a professional cellist, a professor at Wesleyan University, head of advertising for Warner Bros. Motion Pictures and for CBS Entertainment, and director of humanities at the 92nd Street Y in New York City. He is currently Cullen Distinguished Professor of English in the creative writing program at the University of Houston.